JORGITO
Wants to be
HOLY

JORGITO
Wants to be
HOLY

ﬣ

MÓNICA C. ARS

Equipo Familia

2016

First edition, March 2016

Jorgito Wants to be Holy is a translation of *Jorgito quiere ser Santo* © 2015 by Equipo Familia.

ISBN: 978-84-608-6886-6

English translation by Carrie L. Skinner and Mónica C. Ars.

Image on cover: *Divine Innocence*, Charles B. Chambers (1882-1964).

To God for creating me, and to my family for inspiring me.

CHAPTERS

PROLOGUE

Whoever decides to read this book will discover that *Jorgito Wants to be Holy* is a call to restore the family vocation within the Church. Modern times are determined to make us believe that holiness is something from the past and, although Christians count on encountering this opposition, it is worrisome that certain sectors of the Church have also fallen into the consideration that holiness is only for a chosen few.

On the contrary, I argue that raising children to be holy is not only possible but also an exciting adventure. And so, in a world where it is increasingly difficult to educate children in the sacramental life, Christian virtues, and friendship with the great saints Jorgito stands as encouragement along the way. Taking our children to God is the main mission we have as parents and, to achieve it, we certainly need access to divine grace (without which, nothing can be done); but imagination and desire is also required. With these three ingredients, God will prepare a recipe of unique flavor for every Christian family.

The adventures of Jorgito were born on *Adelante la Fe*[*], a traditional Catholic apologetics website that saw light in the year 2014. I decided to write the first article on a cold November night, frustrated by the enormous difficulties I found in the daily struggle to take my children to holiness (both outside and inside the Church). I knew I was not alone. The favorable reception of that article led to a weekly collaboration that lasted for six months. I would like to take this opportunity to publicly thank *Adelante la Fe* for the charming welcome it hosted to Jorgito and his family. Without it, this book would never have seen the light. Also, I can not avoid thanking my older brother, maximum support in

[*]http://www.adelantelafe.com/category/english/

this trance and inspirer of the original idea, and Carrie Skinner who spent some sleepless nights fighting with me over the English translation. This prologue wouldn't be complete without mentioning Ann Cicero and the rest of helpers who kindly took the time to proofread the chapters.

I hope the reader, upon finishing the book, considers this great little family as his own and finds it a source of encouragement in his spiritual struggle. However, I would like to make clear that it is not an autobiography. The stories included in it and the protagonists are fictitious. Naturally, as is easy to guess, many details are taken from my daily family life (with five beautiful children, I have quite a source from which to draw), but the reader should not be tempted to consider them real. It would be great if it were so, and I ask God for that grace.

❧

Chapter One

JORGITO WANTS TO BE HOLY[*]

Amen, I say to you, unless you turn and become like children,
you will not enter the kingdom of heaven. Whoever humbles
himself like this child is the greatest in the kingdom of heaven.
MATTHEW 8:1-4

JORGITO wants to be holy, but the world won't let him. Jorgito is an average six-year-old boy: not very tall, but not too short; not very fair, but not dark, either. As I've said, a typical six-year-old. In fact, Jorgito would pass unnoticed among a crowd of schoolboys... and yet, our hero has something that sets him apart from others; something very important that makes him unique among his generation: *Jorgito wants to be holy.*

When he was a little boy he got into his head the idea of being holy. And if there is something that characterizes our Jorgito, it is that he's a stubborn kid. He gets something into his head and he won't let it go until he gets it done. And of course... with a child like that, this idea could only bring him serious problems.

For how can he become holy in today's world? You might think it's simple: just follow the Catechism, read the gospel, or simply listen to Jesus in prayer. But anyone who says that hasn't really tried to be holy in the world today. Just ask Jorgito.

Jorgito talks to Jesus every night; his parents taught him how when he was very little. He likes to tell Him about his day before yielding to sleep; that's when he seizes the mo-

*Story first published in *Adelante la Fe* on November 10, 2014.

ment to complain about his four brothers, who make his life impossible. Sometimes he even reproaches Him for not making him an only child, but Jesus, with infinite patience, always makes him see that an only child has more difficulty reaching heaven because he can't really learn to share. "And without authentic generosity, you cannot enter heaven," He corrects him fondly.

Jorgito always listens with open ears, because our Jorgito is also a bright child. And he always likes to obey Jesus, although sometimes—the majority of the time—this will cause him real problems. For instance, Jesus told him last week to read the lives of holy saints. "They are little treasures that will guide you," He said as He listed a few interesting biographies such as Saint Martin de Porres, Saint Tarcisius, or Saints Justo and Pastor, patrons of the Diocese of Alcala de Henares.

And Jorgito, who is obedient, did not wait a single day to go to church and ask the priest for these magnificent books. Luckily, the priest who hears him in confession (and who is also beginning to get to know the little boy) is very concerned about his attitude and never misses the opportunity to bring him onto the right path. What would Jorgito do otherwise!

At this point I must clarify that in Jorgito's parish confessionals are not in use because they shoo people away; that's why the priest always greets people in his modern-day office. And our protagonist, who has never seen a confessional, imagines them to be terribly gloomy and dark because it's the only explanation he can find as to why people have never returned to church. What a fright they must have had...!

As the child began to list the readings that Jesus had given him, the priest convulsed in his office chair. A cold sweat ran down our priest's back and the poor man had to wave his hands in order to scare those ideas away. The things Jorgito said!

"Jorgito, forget those stories!" he said condescendingly. "Where do you get such ideas? Lives of saints? You can't be serious! These books tell stories of other times, impossible for man today. You have to read something else; something suitable, profitable, and uplifting."

The priest, perusing through his library, soon found what he wanted: *My Friend, Jesus.* Jorgito, not quite convinced, checked it out and noticed that it was another one of those books that his teachers were determined to give him in religious education class: dull tomes where strange talking sheep taught children to throw papers away so as to keep the city clean.

Our child was not very satisfied, but Jesus told him many times not to talk back to adults, so he left the office in a hurry, feeling sorry for not being able to please his great Friend. As he arrived home, his parents, who were not fools, removed the book from his hands and deposited it on a high shelf so that none of their children could reach it.

At night, when Jesus asked gently if he found the books He recommended to him, Jorgito detailed the conversation with the priest... and the poor child detected an aura of sadness in his Friend.

"Jorgito," Jesus sighed, "let's do this: instead of reading about lives of saints, you will meet them personally. I'm going to ask them to tell you their own stories. What do you think?"

Jorgito was delighted. New friends!

"Jorgito... one more thing."

"Tell me, Lord."

"Don't forget to pray for your priest, all right?"

Again Jorgito detected the profound sadness that frightened him in his Friend and responded as only a six-year-old boy who wants to be holy can respond:

"As you wish, Lord."

Chapter Two

JORGITO AND HALLOWEEN[*]

*Saint Michael the Archangel, defend us in battle. Be our
protection against the wickedness and snares of the Devil. May
God rebuke him, we humbly pray, and do thou, O Prince of the
heavenly hosts, by the power of God, cast into hell Satan, and
all the evil spirits, who prowl about the world seeking the ruin
of souls. Amen.*

LEO XIII

THERE has been a little problem this week at Jorgito's house. It all began last Monday when the teacher sent a note asking parents to bring their children to school dressed for Halloween. Mamá was bothered just by reading it but, as the mother of five that she is, far from showing her irritation, she rose in the face of adversity and found the solution to the problem.

"Mamá, I want to go as a warlock!" suggested the excited Jorgito, without knowing very well what he was saying. "Javi will be a devil, Maria will be a witch, and Antonio will be a skeleton..."

"No, Jorgito," Mamá interrupted decisively. "You will go as Saint Michael."

"As Saint Michael?" Jorgito answered skeptically.

Our Jorgito knew very well who Saint Michael the Archangel was. In fact, he asked for his intercession every night. His question was not meant as an inquiry about the identity of the Archangel, but about the reason for including him

[*]Story first published in *Adelante la Fe* on November 18, 2014.

4

at the school's Halloween party. To Jorgito, that response seemed to lack all logic.

"Of course, honey" responded Mamá skillfully. "Someone has to bring order to the devils. And what did Saint Michael do?" Mamá knew very well the response that her son would give, for she had told him thousands of times. In fact, it was one of her son's favorite stories:

"He expelled the devil from heaven! Well, of course, Mamá! I'll be the envy of the party! I can already picture my friends' faces while I chase them through the playground..."

Mamá knew that her decision would bring problems at school, one more to add to the list. But Mamá is stubborn (as are all mothers of large families) and once she makes a decision, she rarely changes her mind. She searched on Amazon.com (the most convenient store for families that don't have time) for two costumes that could work, a Roman centurion and a Christmas angel, and she combined them wonderfully to create a more than acceptable Saint Michael, the Archangel.

Jorgito's eyes lit up when he saw himself in the mirror. The centurion's uniform looked marvelous on him and the angel's wings were nicely made. He was only missing a sword to complete his outfit, and there Papá intervened to provide the finishing touch of grace. He took a beautiful (plastic) sword from his coat, giving it only after obtaining Jorgito's firm promise not to hit any demons with it.

"All right, at least as long as they pay attention to me, Papá," he responded with an angelical air.

This affirmation was enough for Papá and he entrusted it to him gallantly.

Jorgito marched happily to school, loving the feeling of being the boss. Everything was going well until the teacher asked Jorgito about the reason for his strange attire. And our Jorgito, who knew a lot about this, did not hesitate to give the play-by-play of the expulsion of the devil from the celestial court. This mustn't have humored the teacher much, who became more and more uncomfortable as the story went on. But much worse was the reaction of the rest of the kids in class, when they quickly realized that they represented the band of evil. And, of course, no one likes to feel like a loser... The result was a room full of students crying about the injustice of the whole thing and asking the teacher to remove the abominable makeup from their faces. Jorgito, who found himself on cloud nine, made things even worse by running from side to side, shaking his sentencing sword.

When Mamá returned to pick up our protagonist from school, she was met by a very upset teacher who, nonetheless, was kind enough to call her aside. Once alone, the teacher demanded that next year, she kindly stick to what was asked and find a scary costume for her son. "Like the rest of the world," remarked the teacher.

It was an uncomfortable moment, but a Christian stands up to the world or dies. Mamá opted for the former. Without thinking twice, she responded that if the teacher wanted a costume that evoked fear, she shouldn't worry, because Mamá would dress her son up like one of the four horsemen of the Apocalypse.

Another one of Jorgito's virtues is his intelligence. Therefore, he did not fail to notice the livid face made by his teacher while listening to his mother. Since then, he could not sleep a wink thinking about the fun that next year's Halloween party would bring. If the very mention of this mysterious horseman would make his teacher nearly faint... what would happen with his friends!

At night, once home, after preparing homemade treats to celebrate the feast of All Saints, he climbed into bed to tell Jesus about his day. It was a wonderful surprise when he found the great Saint Michael himself in prayer.

"Hello, Jorgito! I was very proud of you today. You represented me very well."

Jorgito smiled excitedly and thanked him. It was the best end to the day that he could have dreamed of.

"Just one thing, Jorgito. Next time, when you chase after demons, remember to target your teacher too..."

And with a mischievous wink, Saint Michael said goodbye in order to make way for his great Friend, who was anxiously waiting to hear about Jorgito's day.

Chapter Three

JORGITO WANTS TO RECEIVE HIS FIRST COMMUNION[*]

And people were bringing children to him that he might touch them, but the disciples rebuked them. When Jesus saw this he became indignant and said to them, "Let the children come to me; do not prevent them, for the kingdom of God belongs to such as these."

MARK 10:13-15

O NE morning Jorgito rose from his bed resolved to carry out an idea: he would receive his First Communion as soon as he turned seven. His time in prayer with Jesus had become more intimate and one night during a special conversation his great Friend gave him a surprise:

"Jorgito, I want to ask you something."

"Tell me, Lord, I'm listening," he responded expectantly.

"I've been waiting all eternity for the moment when you would receive me in Holy Communion. Would you like to please me? You're almost seven..."

Jorgito's heart leaped. To receive Jesus at the Holy Mass! He had spent years dreaming about it, and now, the Lord Himself was asking him.

"Of course, Lord!" he answered bursting with joy.

"Splendid!" said Jesus, pleased. "Talk to your dad tomorrow. He'll know what to do."

Such as his great Friend had predicted, as soon as Jorgito told his parents about his decision, he obtained their approval.

[*]Story first published in *Adelante la Fe* on November 24, 2014.

8

They both agreed that their son should make his First Communion as soon as possible; he was well prepared (they had already compelled him to learn the Catechism) and they were very conscious of the grace that their son would receive. For this reason, they decided to speak with the priest that very afternoon.

Later that day, Papá picked Jorgito up from school and headed directly to the church; they didn't have any time to lose. They found the priest in his modern-day office, preparing PowerPoint presentations for his homily at the children's Mass on Sunday.

"Good afternoon, Father Antonio," said Papá respectfully.

"Good afternoon, Jorge. What brings you here?"

"I'd like Jorgito to make his Communion on his birthday. He finished studying the Catechism a few months ago and he has asked to receive Jesus..."

The priest had to grab the chair to avoid getting dizzy with fright. First Communion! Jorgito? But he was just barely six. What were these parents thinking?

"Excuse me, Jorge, I don't know if I understand. You're asking me for Jorgito to receive his First Communion this year?" he said very slowly, as if he couldn't even pronounce the words.

"Yes, this year," responded Papá naturally.

The priest dried the cold sweat from his forehead with a handkerchief that rested on top of his office table. That earned him a few seconds to prepare his speech.

"It can't be, Jorge. You're asking something impossible. How could I exempt Jorgito from three years of catechesis? What kind of priest would I be?!..."

Papá feared an answer like this, so he had a response ready.

"Father Antonio, Jorgito knows more than any boy in this parish, and you know it. Ask the boy the Catechism and if he doesn't respond well, we'll end the discussion here."

The priest knew that he'd lost. The months he spent speaking with Jorgito were enough to give him an idea. Essentially, the boy was better prepared than any boy in his first year of catechesis, in his second year... and, truth be told, even up to Confirmation. It was hard to admit, but the father brought him to his knees.

"Yes, yes... but there is also the question of age. Isn't it too soon for a six-year-old boy?" he asked rhetorically.

"Not for Saint Pius X," retorted Papá ably.

Father Antonio wasn't expecting this answer and he regretted underestimating his rival. It was one thing to argue with a parent, but it was another thing entirely to argue against a pope, who also had the annoying condition of having been proclaimed a saint by the Church.

I should have known: "like father like son," he told himself, somewhat annoyed at this family so locked in the past.

"Well, there is also the social aspect of sharing the experience with the rest of the kids..." he rushed to add.

Jorgito's dad is not a man who likes to waste time, so he decided to get straight to the point:

"All right, Father Antonio. If you don't want to let my son make his First Communion as soon as he is seven, I'll find another parish."

That idea put the priest on edge. After all, no priest is happy when his parishioners leave, saying that they have been thrown out of the church.

"Wait! There is no reason to be so extreme," he replied nervously. "We can arrange something: Jorgito will make his First Communion this spring, but first, he will have to join the kids' catechism class in the middle of the course. Then, everyone is happy!"

Father Antonio looked at the father with a triumphal air. He knew that he had kept him at bay: he didn't say no to him, and what he had asked in return was something reasonable. Jorgito would go to catechesis like the rest of the kids. Who knows, this might be the best way of getting rid of the strange ideas that his parents had gotten into his head.

Papá thought about the proposal for an instant. The solomonic solution offered by the priest did not satisfy him, but neither could he find great reasons to oppose. Jorgito still had some months before turning seven... Suddenly, his face lit up with an enormous smile:

"All right, but remember, Father Antonio, you asked for this," Papá answered enigmatically while moving toward the door.

That night, Jorgito told his great Friend about his father's conversation with the priest, and excitedly he confessed being nervous to begin the catechesis along with the rest of the kids. Jesus listened with love but did not hesitate to give a warning:

"Jorgito, do me a favor," He interrupted with great sweetness.

"Yes, Lord?"

"Don't be too harsh with those who don't know..."

Jorgito remained very confused for some time.

"Do you mean the rest of the kids in the class?" he asked confusedly. After all, the other kids had already had two whole years of catechesis, and that made him very nervous. He hoped to be up to their level.

"No, Jorgito..." responded Jesus, amused, "I'm referring to your catechist."

And here He left the matter settled, as bedtime has come for our little boy.

Chapter Four

JORGITO GOES TO CATECHISM CLASS[*]

*At that time Jesus said in reply, "I give praise to you, Father,
Lord of heaven and earth, for although you have hidden these
things from the wise and the learned you have revealed them to
the childlike."*

MATTHEW 11:25

A LL the time spent drawing during Catechism class
disenchanted Jorgito. He thought he was going to
learn many things about the mystery of the Mass,
about the Saints—like his friend Saint Tarcisius, whose defense of the Lord's Body with his own life amazed him—
about the sacraments... but none of this occurred. In fact,
he passed the time coloring hearts for the parish poster that
announced Advent.

"Why do we have to behave well, Juanita?" a girl asked her
catechist, while filling in the last crevices of the photocopied
heart with red paint.

"Because when we behave well, we feel good," she answered, pleased at herself for having expounded such great
wisdom.

"That's pride," Jorgito corrected spontaneously. "If we do
things because they make us feel good, we foster our pride.
We behave well so that we don't hurt Jesus. That's the true
reason!"

Jorgito knew very well what he was talking about; his
great Friend explained it to him one night during prayer. That

[*]Story first published in *Adelante la Fe* on December 1, 2014.

12

day Jorgito's little brother had ruined the homework that he'd worked very hard on and the scene ended with a strong shove that threw the little boy to the ground. Jorgito, during his intimate conversation, confessed to Jesus that he had not acted well at all, but at the same time admitted that it was hard to be sorry.

"He deserved it," he argued with a masterful conviction. "I worked very hard to finish the assignment and my teacher is going to yell at me when I get to class."

Jesus listened attentively—as always—and only when the boy finished his explanation, proceeded to show him the open wounds in His Body.

"Jorgito, when you behave badly, my wounds hurt me a lot. However, if you decide to renounce yourself and bear other people's wrongs for me, my heart is inflamed and the pain is appeased."

Our protagonist was moved by this revelation and since then had kept this reality very present in his life. That's why he responded to the catechist so quickly and naturally. It's the consequences that were the problem...

The kids gave him some teasing, mocking looks. Jorgito said some very odd things! Since he began catechesis in the parish, he had already been in three separate classes. No catechist wanted him in his class!

"Jorgito, what a silly thing to say about pride!" responded a nervous Juanita. "It's important to feel good about oneself. Jesus doesn't want bad things for us..."

The children watched the scene entertained and did not miss the plight of their catechist. It was nice to leave the usual boredom that dominated this weekly hour, and with the arrival of Jorgito the classes were much more amusing. Our boy was going to answer, but a girl beat him to it:

"Well, Jorgito is right. When I cheat on a test and get a good grade, I feel good because I don't get caught... and I don't think that Jesus likes this," she said thoughtfully.

The class clown, who was always looking to cause trouble, quickly took the opportunity and affirmed:

"Well! If I refuse to eat the vegetable soup and if I get my mom to make some fried chicken with baked potatoes, I feel... AWE-SOME!"

The class burst into laughter at the thought; all, of course, except Jorgito and the catechist, whose face grew angrier by the minute. The poor woman grabbed Jorgito by the arm and took him directly to Father Antonio's office.

"I refuse to continue with this boy in my class! It's impossible to deal with him!"

And without another word, she left him abandoned in the office as if he were an annoying pet to deal with. Father Antonio stood looking worried, for there were no more catechism classes where he could put the boy, and right now he couldn't look after him as he was organizing the lighting of the Advent wreath candles in the weekly parish bulletin, which was an impossible task to do. Every year he had to listen to the same complaints of the spiteful parishioners: "If he always chose this catechist to do the lighting in favor of the other, if he agreed on the Jiménez family because they gave more in the collection basket, if he named the worst singer in the choir..." That's why this year he was embracing the idea of doing a "group lighting," even though he was paralyzed by the possibility of starting a fire in the church.

It was then that he noticed Mr. Miguel, the old, serious, and haughty sacristan whom he had inherited from the old priest. Father Antonio didn't understand him; he did his work well—he recognized that—but the man was not involved in the new air that he wanted to give to the parish. It even seemed like he rejected it.

"Yes, I will put him in charge of Jorgito. In short, he cannot make things worse," Father said to convince himself.

He called the sacristan to his office and, with hardly an explanation, put our protagonist in his custody. Mr. Miguel was about to refuse, but Jorgito's deep, worried look made him change his mind at the last second.

"Let's see what you know," said the skeptical sacristan who was sitting on a bench. "Are you a Christian?"

Jorgito's face lit up. How easy! And he answered with a sure voice:

"Yes, I am a Christian by the grace of God."

Mr. Miguel stood amazed. In all his years, he had never received an answer like this...

"What does it mean to be a Christian?" he asked pointedly a second time.

"Being a Christian means being a disciple of Christ," shot Jorgito like a machine gun.

Mr. Miguel looked toward the tabernacle emotionally. Was it possible that after such a long time...?

"Do you know how to pray?" he asked with a certain mistrust.

Jorgito answered by kneeling on the kneeler and prostrating himself before God. The church stood in silence, veiled by two figures kneeling before the tabernacle; and only the angels were witnesses of the tear that slid down the face of the elder while observing the younger from the side.

"Lord, I don't have any friends in my church," Jorgito complained with a foreign bitterness at the presence of his new catechist. "It seems that everything that I do is bad here..."

"Jorgito," his great Friend interrupted sweetly, "this is my house and... how many friends do you see that I have?"

Our protagonist observed that, even though the church was filled with noise coming from the catechism classrooms, the Lord was alone in the church. Nobody paid Him the slightest attention. More, no one seemed to notice His presence. It was then that Jorgito's heart shrank as he understood the meaning of loneliness. What little right he had to complain!

"Lord, at least now you have two friends," he assured Him tenderly while looking at his new mentor.

At that moment, someone touched his shoulder. It was time to finish; his father had come to pick him up. Mr. Miguel got up from the bench to meet his father.

"My name is Miguel. I'm going to be your son's catechist," he commented with a broken voice, "and from what I have seen, I think that it's going to be a true honor."

Jorge observed him for a moment and with resoluteness, gave a strong handshake; one that felt like minority, resistance, catacombs, and... authenticity.

Chapter Five

JORGITO AND ADVENT[*]

And suddenly there was with the angel a multitude of the
heavenly host, praising God and saying: "Glory to God in the
highest and on earth peace to men of good will."

LUKE 2, 13:14

J ORGITO had lived the first week of Advent a bit pensive. On Sunday he woke up and discovered that the table, any other day covered by hot chocolate cups and freshly baked cookies, now remained naked, crowned only by four humble candles. His parents waited patiently for their five children to be seated so that they could explain the change in menu.

"Today begins a very important season for Christians," announced Papá solemnly, "the beginning of Advent, the time to prepare for the birth of Jesus."

The kids stirred restlessly, knowing what he was referring to. They all liked Christmas; it was a time filled with happiness: vacations, holiday carols, and Grandma's Christmas cookies. Jorgito's stomach growled remembering the homemade anise cookies they made with Grandma on Christmas Eve.

"It is a time of grace," Papá continued, "but we should be attentive, otherwise it will pass unnoticed."

Our protagonist looked at Papá with inquisitive eyes. "How could it be possible to miss Christmas!? The whole world spoke about it!" Papá smiled, gazing at his son; the

---

[*]Story first published in *Adelante la Fe* on December 9, 2014.

depth of Jorgito's look confirmed that he would be capable of understanding his explanation.

"The world doesn't want Jesus to be born. It doesn't need Him. That's why it offers us noise, gifts, and food so that we forget about Him. It is easy to fall into the trap if we're not careful." Jorgito tried to understand his father, but he didn't get it. It was impossible!

It was then that his guardian angel decided to intervene by reminding him about the grocery store. Last Thursday, our protagonist went grocery shopping with his mother and decided to buy a chocolate Advent calendar. Motivated by an impulse, he quickly grabbed it from the shelf and asked permission to put it in the cart. His mother glanced at it, but returned it to its place sadly.

"I'm sorry, Jorgito, but this calendar does not represent Christmas. There is no baby Jesus, no Mary, no Saint Joseph. It's ridiculous!"

It didn't take the boy's critical sense (despite being less developed because of his age) long to get the idea: a red-nosed reindeer, covered by an absurd Santa hat, appeared smiling on the cover.

"Let's do this, Dear. If we find a calendar that has a true Christmas spirit, we'll buy it!"

Jorgito left running down the aisle ready to claim his trophy... but the disappointment still lasted when he got in the car. He had not found anything.

"Another time, Jorgito."

His guardian angel had been sharp in remembering this and that's why the boy, even though not understanding completely, sensed what Papá was trying to explain.

"Then, how do we prepare?" inquired his older brother.

"The Church offers three rules: prayer, fasting, and almsgiving."

"Like during Lent?" he responded surprised.

Papá was happy about the comment and quickly offered an answer:

"Why invent new things if what we have works perfectly?"

The morning remained busy in making plans for Advent and the family reached some compromises: to go more frequently to the tabernacle; to visit the elderly who lived in the village—increasingly more alone as the youth fled to the city; to eliminate treats; to have Mary closer in thought; and to improve the family choir enough to offer the Lord a Christmas carol (unfortunately, dear Reader, the Lord hasn't granted this family the gift of intonation). Additionally, every Sunday, Papá, as head of the family and in order to eliminate unending discussions about "why did he get to light it instead of me," would light one candle to remind them that the great day was one week closer.

All the members compromised on something; no one wanted to lose sight of the very important event that was about to occur, and they concluded the meeting by asking the Lord the grace to carry it out (as we know, there's always a risk of becoming Pelagian). That day there was no hot chocolate and cookies, for they had just committed to restricting treats during Advent.

Since then, Jorgito began executing his own plan for Advent. What cost him most, as always, was tolerating his brothers. They could be so annoying! He loved them madly, but sometimes—most of the time—they pushed him to the limit. The holy patience that Saint Teresa loved to mention disappeared many times from Jorgito's house and our protagonist, in spite of searching, was unable to bring it back.

At the church, our boy was found in the pew telling Jesus about his circumstance. Mr. Miguel, who had been teaching him the mysteries of the altar during his catechism class, had left him alone in prayer for ten minutes. "The most important thing that I can teach you, Jorgito, is this," he said, pointing toward the tabernacle while he went to the sacristy.

Jorgito took advantage of the moment until his prayer was interrupted by some light taps on the shoulder. Surprised, he lifted his head and looked into the face of the girl from his last catechism class who had come to his defense.

"What are you doing, Jorgito?" she asked, thinking it strange to see him kneeling and alone.

"Praying" he responded naturally.

The girl did not expect this answer, thinking that he had been punished. Jorgito had not fit into any of the catechism classes but, nonetheless, she liked him. There was something in that boy that powerfully captured her attention.

"Why are you kneeling?" she asked, intrigued.

Our protagonist did not understand her question, given that, to him, it was something that went without saying. Nonetheless, Jesus had told him many times that he could not be unkind with others, and so he decided to answer.

"Look at Jesus," he said while he pointed toward the crucifix. "Right now he is nailed to the cross. Kneeling is the least that I can do to be with Him. It doesn't seem right to take any other position."

The girl, intrigued, focused her gaze on the crucified Jesus. Never before had she thought about Jesus this way. She studied His wounds, the blood coming from His rib, his contrite face... and for the first time in her life, really contemplated Jesus on the cross. Suddenly, she felt a tremendous need to kneel together with Jorgito.

"And now what do I do?" she asked him, she herself now kneeling in the pew.

"Then you talk to him. He likes it very much when we tell him everything. Jesus is always waiting for us."

The girl did not understand everything, but nonetheless she decided to trust her new friend. She looked at the crucifix and started to pray.

"Don't look there," interrupted our protagonist. "It's better to look there (pointing toward the tabernacle). Jesus is really present in the tabernacle. Why waste time with an image if we have Him before our eyes?"

Our girl smiled and obeyed him. After all, Jorgito said many logical things. Then it became silent. Well, not completely silent... because the walls of the church boomed from the sound of the catechism classes practicing their Christmas carols. But this time, heaven and earth were in agreement because, in the celestial court, the angels and the Saints also sang with joy. Teaching someone what they do not know is a work of mercy... and Jorgito, by his work, had made the crucified Jesus smile.

Chapter Six

JORGITO AND FATHER ALFONSO[*]

[The Mass] is the most beautiful thing this side of heaven. It came forth out of the grand mind of the Church and lifted us out of earth and out of self, and wrapped us round in a cloud of mystical sweetness and the sublimities of a more than angelic liturgy, [...] and charmed us with celestial charming so that our very senses seemed to find vision, hearing, fragrance, taste and touch more than ear can give.

FATHER FREDERICK FABER

JORGITO couldn't wait for Sunday to arrive. Papá and Mamá had decided to visit an old priest, Father Alfonso. The priest's current location could be found far from home, hidden in the mountains, and no less than one hour by car. There had been much talk about why he was stationed out there. The new bishop, a few months after his arrival, rewarded Father Alfonso's work in defense of tradition with a so-called "promotion" which was located at an altitude of about 3,600 feet in a small, practically unpopulated village.

There, he had only a few old ladies as parishioners to tend to; but Father Alfonso was happy because, for the first time in his life, he had time to write and could spend much time in front of the tabernacle. In addition, since the town's little old ladies were illiterate, they had asked him to say the Mass in Latin like they had learned it as children. Until then, they had not been successful in getting any priest to pay attention to their request since they were usually sent priests fresh out of the seminary—always wishing to leave that post—but when

---

[*]Story first published in *Adelante la Fe* on December 15, 2014.

they saw Father Alfonso arrive, whose white head of hair bore the mark of time, they did not think twice.

For the priest, the first time that he heard the *Confiteor* in his new church, his heart almost burst. The Lord knew how to do all things very well!

In addition, not only had his prayer life been revitalized, but he had succeeded in gaining some necessary extra weight too. Of course the fault was with the little old ladies, who fought to have him as a guest in their homes. As soon as it occurred to one to kill a rabbit for stew, the other, who found out, fattened a chicken to cook it. They cooked wonderfully!

But what Father Alfonso liked most, without a doubt, was *tocino de cielo*, a dessert that they prepared with free range eggs. He hadn't expressed this to any of his parishioners, but the feminine intuition—excellently used in this case—had managed to pick up on his preference. The health of the priest was improving a lot in the last months, surely because in this little town, the term "cholesterol" was completely unknown.

Father Alfonso had left his old parish with few words, leaving in the same way as he had arrived; but without intending to, he had made a strong mark on some parishioners. Papá and Mamá were among them; so much so that they did not hesitate to visit him from time to time to remember the old times and make sure that he was well—something that, by the way, his old bishop, now retired, also did.

On this occasion, his parents had chosen the feast of the Immaculate Conception to make a visit. To Jorgito, the trip seemed to take an eternity, having long since lost count of the curves on the road! But he was eager to see Father Alfonso again; he was the one who had taught him to spend time in front of the tabernacle, who had spoken to him about the virtues of the Saints, and the one who was going to teach him all that was necessary to be an altar boy... It's a shame he had to change parishes before having that chance!

That's why, when they parked the car outside the door, he shot out of the car toward the church.

"Father Alfonsoooooo! Father Alfonsooooo!" he shouted at the top of his lungs while crossing through the town.

Needless to say, the townspeople knew the instant Jorgito's family arrived. Excited, they came running from their houses to greet the family. The arrival of kids in town was always a cause of joy and, in this case, we must bear in mind that five children came all at one stroke. This situation detained Jorgito's parents a bit, who, politely, paid attention to all the neighbors.

Our boy, meanwhile, arrived at the church, finding it to be open. How strange! It was so difficult to find an open church in the city! Without delay, though with a certain care, he stuck his head inside and found Father Alfonso on his knees in the pew. The boy was not surprised; he remembered him like this, always kneeling in prayer. How many times he had to wait for Father Alfonso to finish praying! "The first thing, Jorgito: prayer. The second: prayer. The rest... comes along" he used to say.

The boy entered the church, knelt before God, and tiptoed toward his friend. As Father Alfonso did not get up, he decided to kneel next to him. There he remained a long while. Finally, the priest looked up from the gospel that he had in his hands and stroked the boy's hair.

"Come on! Let's go outside," he said in a whisper.

The priest rose from the pew and walked toward the exit. Jorgito could not help but admire the appearance of the priest. The cassock, that he had not seen since he left, gave Father Alfonso a solemnity that was hard to find in Father Antonio. Both were priests, but...

"Good morning, Father Alfonso!" exclaimed Papá, who began to walk toward the entrance.

"Good morning, family!" he responded with joy. "It's been a long time! Forgive me for not coming to greet you, but I was preparing my homily."

Jorgito could not avoid making comparisons: Father Antonio always prepared his homily in front of the computer; on the other hand, Father Alfonso preferred doing so in front of the tabernacle. So many things had changed since he left!

Our protagonists continued speaking until it was time for Mass. Father Alfonso told them that he was going to celebrate according to the old rite, "like my four parishioners have requested," and he handed them a missal so that they could follow along. This intrigued Jorgito very much. "What would this old rite be like?" he said to himself while they took a seat.

He did not have time to ask many questions, since the priest, dressed in solemn vestments, processed to the altar:

"*Introibo ad altare Dei...*"

Jorgito marvelled at what he saw. He didn't understand the words, but he did understand the meaning of what was taking place. The priest looked toward the altar, toward God! There were long periods of silence during the celebration (which, by the way, he used to pray and to ask God to care for all of his family and friends); he listened with astonishment to that unknown language and paid attention, spellbound, to the moment of consecration. At Communion time, Jorgito was impressed to see everybody kneeling. How beautiful!

It seemed that the whole family agreed with his opinion, including even the littlest ones; maybe because they did not have the distraction of the guitar, they behaved well. When Mass ended, our protagonist was overwhelmed by what had happened during that hour. It's not that it felt short (that would be asking too much for his age) but that it seemed much shorter than when Father Antonio officiated.

Finishing the Divine Office, the family went to eat at the house of one of the parishioners. There they confirmed Father Alfonso's claims about the the culinary gifts of the villagers. Everything was so tasty!

In the end, and with sadness, as is true of all the good things in this world, the time to leave arrived.

"Jorgito, I am very sorry not to have been able to dedicate some time to you alone," lamented the priest.

In that moment, our protagonist wanted to tell him that it was not his fault; that he had learned more in a day than in many months. He also wanted to thank him for everything that he had taught him, telling him not to worry, that he was well... so many things!

But he couldn't, for we must remember that he was only six years old. Instead, he ran to Father Alfonso to give him a warm and emotional hug. At other times, our priest would have turned him aside discreetly, but this time he understood that it was one of God's caresses, and allowed it. The wisdom of old age!

When they were already buckled into the car, Papá remembered the gift that they had brought him. He left the car and gave Father Alfonso a little book.

"I think that you will like this a lot. I know that now you have time to read."

Father Alfonso waved to them, and only when the car was lost among the zigzags of the roads, looked at the book. The first thing that he noticed was that the author was a priest who had the same name as he did. And the title, *The Mystery of Prayer*. Knowing the family, it was very clear that the book would be worthwhile.

Chapter Seven

JORGITO HAS TWO MOTHERS[*]

*When Jesus saw his mother and the disciple there whom he
loved, he said to his mother, "Woman, behold, your son." Then
he said to the disciple, "Behold, your mother." And from that
hour the disciple took her into his home.*

JOHN 19:26-27

JORGITO is a fortunate child and he knows it: he has two
mothers. This circumstance should not be particular to
Jorgito and his family, but looking around, it's something
that only they seem to know.

Jorgito has his mother on earth, who loves him like crazy
and takes care of him; but also and more importantly, he has
Mary, his mother in heaven who loves him even more. In
the beginning, it was hard to believe what his earthly mother
told him, "Jorgito, I love you very much, very, very much;
but Mary loves you still more." But as he and his siblings
got older, he began to understand. The fact is that whenever
Mamá lost her patience with them (which was something
rather frequent), whenever she did not give them the attention that she should (according to the world's standards), or
whenever she suddenly felt the temptation to fail them, she
would solemnly announce:

"My children: where Mamá can't reach, Mary can!"

She said this so many times (because even though Mamá
is a Supermamá, we should not forget that she has five little
ones and this is like having kryptonite in the house) that her

[*]Story first published in *Adelante la Fe* on December 22, 2014.

little ones internalized it perfectly. For this reason, Jorgito is fortunate. When he feels alone at school because he has had a fight with his best friend, he goes to Mary and tells her. When his earthly mother is not able to speak with him, he doesn't hesitate to share his doubts with her. When the devil tempts him and makes him embarrassed to share something with his great Friend, the first thing that he does is open his heart to his mother in heaven. After all, Mary is a mother who is available twenty-four hours a day!

But, without a doubt, the funniest thing of all is the adults' reaction at the park. When they ask about his mother, the first thing that he says is:

"Which one? Because... I have two."

And the people reward him with a tolerant, understanding smile. At least, until they ask more questions in the moments that follow and our protagonist speaks about his heavenly mother, because then, they leave scandalized with their children (especially if they last long enough to hear the part where he says, "the one who loves me the most is my mother in heaven").

Jorgito doesn't understand this behavior, but he has already become accustomed to it. And when Mamá is not around, he tells Mary. Then, the Virgin with the utmost sadness tells him:

"Ah, Jorgito! I understand the parents of the world less all the time... Why don't they want me for their children?"

This afternoon our boy was found playing with his siblings in the park. Another good thing about having so many brothers is that they can fill the park with their presence alone. Because of this, they have a wonderful time even though there are no other kids around. They remained here for an hour until a girl from catechism class arrived with whom he had become good friends.

"Hi, Sara! What are you doing here? I've never seen you in this park."

Sara, without notice, began to cry.

"What's wrong?" Jorgito asked, worried.

The girl wiped the tears from her face and with effort was able to overcome her emotion long enough to tell him her problem:

"This week I'm with my dad. And it's not that I don't like to be with him, but that I miss my mom."

Jorgito didn't need any more information. He perfectly understood what was happening. Unfortunately, and even though children should live in a world where the selfishness of divorce does not exist, it was a very present reality in the school environment of our protagonist.

"I see," he said without adding much more, because what could he say to someone who felt motherless?

Jorgito's guardian angel, anxious, began jumping around him: "You know the answer, you know it!" But this time his intervention was not necessary. Jorgito knew it too.

"Why don't you talk to Mary?" he suggested.

"To Mary Jiménez? But if she doesn't know where I live..." she answered a bit confused, thinking that he was referring to one of her classmates from catechism class.

Jorgito laughed at the remark. "What things you say, Sara! I'm talking about the Virgin Mary, our mother in heaven. She's always with us! And she cares for us marvelously!"

Sara was confused. She didn't know what he was talking about. Mary was the mother of Jesus. At Christmas they sang her some carols; in May they brought her flowers during their catechism class... but that's it. No one had said anything about Mary also being her mother.

Jorgito understood his new friend's doubts. He remained silent for a while, deciding how to explain it to her:

"Mary is Jesus' gift to all the children in the world. She is our mother in heaven and cares for each one of us with a special sweetness. Although we can't see her, she is watching over us! Because of this, I always turn to her when I need her." Jorgito saw that she was listening attentively, so he decided to make himself sound interesting. "Can I tell you a secret?"

"What?" she responded intrigued.

"She has never failed me."

Sara appreciated Jorgito's words. "A mother? That was always there?" But on the other hand, she felt a twinge in her heart.

"And your mom doesn't get jealous? I don't want her to think that I have replaced her..."

Jorgito began to shake his head back and forth vigorously.

"Come on! My mom is the one who reminds me of her presence once and again. What mother doesn't want the best mother that has ever existed to look after her children?"

Sara nodded thoughtfully. She began to like the idea of having another mother in this way, to whom she could turn when she was feeling lonely, sad, or even happy.

"Jorgito, will she listen to me?" she asked fearfully, "because I never paid attention to her before; maybe she will be angry."

"She would not be the best mother in the world if she did not listen," he said with conviction.

Our little girl was full of joy. She was going to ask him about many more doubts, but her father didn't gave her the chance. He grabbed her and carried her away when he saw her speaking with Jorgito. He didn't like the boy, for he said many strange things.

Sara, before her father took her, shouted to Jorgito:

"Thanks a lot! You have given me the best Christmas gift!"

Jorgito was surprised for he hadn't given her anything.

"I did?" he responded, stunned.

"Yes, a new mother," she responded joyfully.

Chapter Eight

JORGITO EXCLAIMS: "ENOUGH!"*

Whoever causes one of these little ones who believe in me to sin,
it would be better for him to have a great millstone hung
around his neck and to be drowned in the depths of the sea.

MATTHEW 18:6

JORGITO found himself in the park with his siblings during the cold Christmas Eve morning. While Grandma and Mamá prepared dinner, Papá took them out for a while. It is a great day for Jorgito. He really likes celebrating Christmas Eve with his family, and more, this year the Christmas carol that he has prepared with his siblings doesn't sound too bad. Because of this, it all points to a good Christmas bonus, and although the money that they'll collect will be destined for charity, it is still quite a sight to watch the shepherd's pouch fill up with coins.

While trying to catch his older brother, a voice called him from behind:

"Hi, Jorgito!"

"Hi, Esteban!" he replied, happy to see a classmate. "Aren't you excited about Christmas Eve?"

"A little... I guess," said his friend with a certain amount of indifference.

"Only a little?"

Jorgito was amazed. Christmas Eve was the best night of the year! And Esteban had much to celebrate tonight, be-

---

*Story first published in *Adelante la Fe* on December 29, 2014.

cause the Lord was giving him a little brother in a few months. He was excited not to be an only child anymore!

Jorgito spent weeks explaining to him that the best thing about having a baby in the house is the day he laughs for the first time. That's when you realize how much fun you'll have with him. And babies always smell marvelous, well, except when they spit up, but fortunately that's what mamá and papá are for. He also recommended that he feed him a bottle and finally, very prudently, advised him to be far away when his mom changes the baby's diaper after eating solid food for the first time.

"But you should be excited!" he said cheerfully. "This year you are going to have a baby in the house, like baby Jesus!"

Esteban remained silent for a moment, not knowing what to say. It was awkward. Finally, he muttered:

"I'm not going to have a little brother. The doctors told my mom that something wasn't right and my parents say that *'It's cruel to bring a child like that into the world.'* So, well... I don't have a little brother anymore."

Jorgito felt like he had been kicked in the stomach. He had the wind knocked out of him. Esteban realized this and defended himself:

"It's OK. So now I'll remain an only child! My mom and dad say that I am very lucky, because I will have them all to myself."

Our protagonist wanted to tell his friend to stop talking. Every word that was said pierced his heart a little more. Jorgito knew very well what Esteban's parents had done. It had been a long time since his parents had explained the cruel reality of abortion. His own mother had to stand up to a doctor who wanted an amniocentesis because his sister appeared to have a cyst on her head. From then on, they always prayed the fourth mystery of the rosary for those mothers who had an abortion or for those who were thinking about it. And every time they walked by an abortion "clinic" near the house, they observed a moment of silent mourning until they had passed by that place. How awful!

But, in spite of everything, Jorgito had never experienced this reality up close.

"I want to go home. I don't feel well," pleaded a nauseated Jorgito.

His friend remained repentantly quiet and, understanding Jorgito's reaction—they had spoken too much about his future little brother to ignore it—began to walk away silently, full of shame.

Already at home, Jorgito, in tears, threw himself into his mother's lap and, with great horror, explained what was wrong. Mamá, very serious, bent down to his level and said:

"Look at the Nativity. What do you see?"

The boy wiped the tears from his eyes and looked at the family's Nativity scene. The straw cradle was empty. Jesus had not been born yet. Tonight Papá, after blessing the Christmas dinner, would place the Infant Jesus in His crib.

"It's missing the baby Jesus," he responded between sobs.

"Exactly! And why do you think we celebrate His birth tonight? Why do you think that we sing 'The Savior has been Born'? Why are Christians so full of joy on this special night?"

Mamá waited patiently so that he could reflect; she wasn't in any hurry. Meanwhile, Jorgito thought about the terrible sin of Esteban's parents; then, he also thought about his own sins. He thought about the pain his great Friend must have suffered on that horrible day when those parents made their decision and about how much pain He must feel because of all of the terrible sins of the world.

"The Savior has been born..." he carefully muttered the words of the Christmas carol.

"Jorgito, we rejoice because God, in spite of everything, loves us. And He sends His Son to save us from our sins.

We can find forgiveness in the Lord, even forgiveness from this atrocious sin. We only have to seek it. Isn't it incredible? Christmas Eve is intimately linked to the Passion and cannot be understood without it. Thanks to the birth of Jesus, there is redemption for humanity. Do you understand?"

Jorgito looked at the Nativity... until then he had not understood. Now he understood a little, because we should not forget that the birth of God still remains a great mystery for mankind.

When Jorgito turned around, Mamá wasn't there. She had left him alone with his thoughts.

At Midnight Mass, our protagonist remembered to pray for the children who died by the cruel crime of abortion and also for their mothers. When he was going to bed his mom asked him if he was feeling better.

"It still hurts when I breathe," he responded honestly.

"That's the sign of a Christian, Jorgito. We are bound to the suffering of the cross. The day that you don't feel pain is the day that you have put down your cross. On that day, you should worry!" Mamá remained silent for a moment and then continued, "the world wants you to run from suffering, but don't forget that Jesus was crucified, and we are all called to live in Him, to live like Him."

Mamá gave him a warm kiss on the forehead and tucked him in. Jorgito smiled sadly and a tear slid down his cheek when he returned to the thought of that little boy. But he also remembered Jesus, recently born in the stable, and his heart cast off the bitterness. How great is God that He was born for our sins!

"The Savior has been born..." was the final verse that he sang to the Baby Jesus before he fell asleep.

Meanwhile, at the same time in Esteban's house, a cry could be heard:

"What happened, Esteban?" asked his mother while running to his room.

The boy had woken up from a terrible nightmare: he dreamed that his parents had thrown him out of the house because he had not gotten good grades, because he was not handsome enough, or because he did not behave himself well enough.

"Nothing, Mom," he said between sobs. "Nothing."

His mom returned, worried, to the kitchen; Esteban had wet the bed several nights.

"Don't worry, Dear, it's only a cry for attention. Children are like that," explained her husband, trying to downplay the issue without knowing why, while drying the empty glasses of champagne that had been drunk during dinner.

Chapter Nine

JORGITO EXPERIENCES AN ALTERNATIVE CHRISTMAS*

But we hold this treasure in earthen vessels, that the surpassing power may be of God and not from us. We are afflicted in every way, but not constrained; perplexed, but not driven to despair; persecuted, but not abandoned; struck down, but not destroyed; always carrying about in the body the dying of Jesus, so that the life of Jesus may also be manifested in our body...

2 CORINTHIANS 4:7-10

MAMÁ is worried. Since Jorgito returned to school after the holidays, she noticed that he's been somewhat crestfallen and absentminded. She mentioned this to her husband and they decided to organize a family trip to the mountains. Anyone who has children knows that you have to provide the opportunity for a child to speak his mind and be patient while he does so. That's why Mamá laughs openly at those television series where busy parents manage to talk to their offspring in a matter of minutes; no child opens up so easily...!

Because of it, on this sunny Saturday morning, we find Jorgito's family hiking in the mountains. The first thing that they do is pray the rosary. *"Hail Mary, full of grace"* is echoed through the landscape. Jorgito looks up to heaven and knows that Mary is pleased; she has rewarded them with such a beautiful day! Suddenly, a frightened partridge, alerted by the noise, flees from its hideout and makes the whole family laugh. How much does the little one enjoy nature!

*Story first published in *Adelante la Fe* on January 14, 2015.

37

With the rosary finished, Papá seizes the moment to talk with the boy. Mamá quietly steps away and leaves them alone. Father and son then chat about divine and human things: the Christmas anecdotes, the birth of Jesus, the last book they read together, plans for next summer... And only after Papá sees that Jorgito has relaxed does he decide to address the issue.

"Jorgito, Mamá noticed that you are distant these days. What's wrong?" he asks fondly.

Jorgito remains deep in thought for a few seconds and then answers:

"On Wednesday we had to write an essay about what we did this Christmas..." he began, trailing off without finishing his thought. "My friends did so many things: going to movies at the theater, riding the Christmas train, a visit to Santa Claus at the mall, the musicals... I," he said ashamed, "didn't do any of that."

Papá waited patiently; the boy was not yet finished.

"When I told the class I spent the holidays in the village and that I dared to gather eggs at the farmyard... They laughed at me! And then, there's the matter of presents: all my friends received so many! Even a PlayStation, Papá!" he said with bitterness.

Papá understood at once what was wrong. He thought about his answer for a while and, after asking Saint Joseph's help, decided to ask him an intriguing question:

"Jorgito, what would you prefer to be: a mouse's head or a lion's tail?"

Our boy didn't expect this kind of answer and his eyes became wide open. What did his father have in mind with this question? Head of a mouse? Tail of a lion?

"I don't understand, Papá," he asserted, trying to gain some time. Papá wasn't going to make things easy for the boy.

"It's a question that my father asked of me many years ago. Now, it's your turn to answer it."

Jorgito was about to explode with excitement. Grandpa asked that same question of Papá, which meant it had to be very important! Our boy started to think. At first, he preferred to be a head rather than a simple tail. Who wouldn't? But then, he also thought that it would be better to be a lion than a mouse... It was a hard decision to make; Papá had made things difficult!

"I don't know, Papá!" he responded nervously.

"Let's see, Jorgito: do you prefer to be the first among the weak or the last among the strong?"

This response cleared things up a bit for our boy. That's what Papá meant! Then, he knew the answer:

"I'd rather be a lion's tail," he proclaimed with a serious voice.

Papá smiled pleased.

"That's the same thing I told your grandfather."

The little boy thought at that moment he was going to levitate like his friend Saint Paschal Baylon.

"Jorgito, your friends seem to stand out because they went to many places during Christmas, had many 'experiences,' and received many gifts... But, Jorgito, your friends are mice."

The boy was left speechless. Papá had been very convincing.

"They don't know how to enjoy the tranquility of a day; they need to have continuous experiences in order to amuse themselves... But if you look into them you'll notice they're empty. They've gone to the theater so many times that they don't enjoy it. They finish one movie and are already thinking about the next one. It's not a novelty, it's a right. They watch the Christmas parade, but they don't know that Santa Claus represents Saint Nicholas or the reason they receive presents. They think it's because they deserve them..."

Jorgito nodded. That was true! During the Christmas parade, he met some friends who didn't know that Santa Claus was in fact Saint Nicholas, famous for his secret gift-giving.

Papá continued:

"They celebrate Christmas, not knowing why. How many friends have you seen at Mass these days?"

The boy remembered how bitterly Father Antonio had complained during New Year's Mass because hardly anyone had gone... and no other children except he and his brothers!

"And if you scratch a bit, you will see how weak and skittish they really are. They're not used to suffering. They have it all done for them. Do you remember when I asked you and your brother to pick up the garbage that some stray dogs had scattered all over the farm house?"

Of course he remembered! They had such a hard time doing it! They had to put on some gloves to pick up all the smelly and rotten garbage... It smelled so bad they had to take turns in order not to vomit. How happy they felt when they finished!

"Do you think your friends would have done it?"

The boy laughed to himself. Even his friend Pepe refused to pick up a paper from the ground, arguing that he hadn't thrown it!

"Right now you're small, Jorgito, and you're only a tail of a lion. But, as you get older, what do you think you'll become?"

Jorgito felt overjoyed and wanted to know what Mamá thought.

"Mamá, what do you think of all of this?"

"It's easy, honey. I married a true lion," she answered proudly.

The whole family laughed at the comment and continued the hike. Jorgito wasn't sad anymore. He ran among the bushes with a sword that he made from a stick. He felt like a powerful conquistador reconquering Spain.

"For the glory-y-y-y-y-y!" He yelled, his words echoing from one side of the mountain to another.

Papá, amused, had another great idea:

"How about if we design our own flag? Since we're a strange family, let's make a symbol that identifies us."

Needless to say, the idea was a great success. As soon as they reached home they started drawing. The result: a huge tailed lion with a cross on the chest, surrounded by twelve stars and set in a blue background in honor of Mary. Papá drew it carefully on paper and decided to order it on the Internet. It would be a late Christmas present.

At night, before falling asleep, Jorgito started to pray:

"Hello, Lion!" said Jesus with love, responding to his calling.

"You heard us this morning?" asked the child surprised.

"Jorgito, I always listen."

"Then, what do you think of all of this?" he asked with curiosity. "Your father is right. You won't reach holiness by chance. You'll need many virtues and, sadly, the world doesn't foster them anymore. Listen to your parents, Jorgito, and don't be afraid to be different. Become a real lion for me!"

Jorgito slept that night comforted. He didn't feel strange anymore; he dreamed about his family's new flag, the reconquering of Spain, his wish for holiness... "For the glory!" was the last thing he thought of while his flag waved proudly along the horizon of his dreams.

Chapter Ten

JORGITO AND THE VIRTUE OF EFFORT

Do not fear: I am with you; do not be anxious: I am your God.
I will strengthen you, I will help you, I will uphold you with
my victorious right hand.

ISAIAH 41:10

"MAMÁ, it's not fair!" exclaimed Jorgito while entering the house.

Mamá hung his coat on the rack and observed that the child was very worked up.

"What happened?"

"It's my English teacher! She gives us so much work. There are times when we can't even finish it. And on top of that, even when we do, she gives very low grades." Jorgito could not stop talking. "This morning she asked me the lesson, and since she was only speaking in English, I didn't understand her. She gave me an F on my assignment and made me take my seat. It's not fair!"

Mamá listened respectfully but remained silent. It's true that the teacher was demanding, even more if compared with the rest of Jorgito's teachers. But this did not mean she was unfair. Mamá knew from her own experience, as she had also suffered demanding teachers in her life.

"I understand..."

"Pablo's mom said that she was going to speak with the principal about her, because a teacher has no right to treat her students that way."

"She has no right?" repeated Mamá paraphrasing his words. "Where did you learn this expression?"

"Well, from Pablo."

"Ah... I see!" she said, thoughtfully.

"And Sara's parents, María's and Julián's too."

"What? Them too?" said the woman lost in her thoughts.

"Maybe you should also complain to the principal. Are you listening to me?"

Mamá waited patiently for Jorgito to put his backpack in his room before responding. What the boy was saying made sense. Some weeks earlier, many parents were complaining after school about this teacher; even on Facebook and Twitter. But if it is true that Jorgito brought a lot of English homework home, it was also true that the teacher took the time to correct it, explaining the errors and demanding more.

It had been a long time since Jorgito's parents had met a teacher of this calibre. Lately, the teachers had succumbed to the fashion of prohibiting homework, so typical of this modern society: "that a child needs to rest, that the parents don't have time to do homework with their children, that it deprives children of creativity..." And the teachers, tired of enduring the parents' complaints, had succumbed to the pressure. Because of this, the quality of classroom instruction (in both knowledge and requirements) had been lowered exponentially in recent years.

It was in this system that Jorgito (and ninety percent of the class) was used to getting wonderful grades, that was true; but without any effort. For this reason, having an "old school" teacher had presented a great challenge to the boy, and it was costing him to overcome it.

"Let's see, dear. Have you been given a grade that you didn't deserve?"

"Well..." the boy tried to remember, but he couldn't come up with an example. "But it's because she doesn't give me time to finish all the assignments, and because I lose points for every spelling error, and because she doesn't like the mess of the eraser marks, and..."

"Then," interrupted Mamá, "as I see it, she's more of a demanding teacher than an unfair one. Why is that so bad?"

Jorgito opened his mouth to complain, but ultimately suppressed his words. There are times when he would like his parents to be more like those of his friends: more understanding.

"Jorgito, life is not always rosy; in fact, it rarely is. A good teacher is one who actually teaches. And, without effort, without striving, you'll never learn a thing. Your teacher asks a lot of you, but she also asks a lot of herself. How long do you think it takes her to correct your assignments?"

The boy remembered all the corrections that she put in his notebook: spelling errors, blurs, wrong answers, poorly expressed ideas...

"A long time, Mamá," he realized sorrowfully.

"And, don't you think it would be easier for her to do the same as the rest of the teachers?"

"Well... yes."

"Then, why doesn't she do it?"

Jorgito went to his room angry. Mamá's response wasn't what he'd hoped for; he would have liked a little support, but deep down he knew that there was a reason.

That evening in prayer, he was hardly able to concentrate because of the English assignment.

"What's wrong, Jorgito?" asked Jesus.

The boy explained the disappointment that he'd suffered with his mother and the demands of his teacher. Jesus listened interestedly until Jorgito was finished and then spoke:

"Jorgito, do you know the parable of the talents?"

"Yes, it's the one that tells the story of a master who leaves his estate. Before he goes, he entrusts his money to three of his servants.

"That's the one. And what happened?"

"Well, two servants are able to increase the money. The third, however, is afraid and hides the money. When the master returns, he is upset with the third servant because he wasn't able to produce any more than what he had in the beginning."

"Very good! And what does this parable tell you?"

"Ummm... I don't know."

"Come on, Jorgito! You can do better. Try again."

"That it is necessary to try really hard and make a serious effort?"

"Very good! And now the more difficult question. Why?"

The boy shrugged his shoulders.

"Jorgito, love demands effort. Without sacrifice, without sweat, without determination, you can't speak about love. It would only be an absurd illusion. Sooner or later, if you want to follow me, you will need the virtues of constancy, perseverance, and tenacity. The road is difficult... Ah, if parents only knew! The virtues require practice, and because of this you cannot complain about your teacher. Rather, treat her with love and try to pay attention. Can you do it?"

Our protagonist listened attentively and, although not understanding entirely, decided to trust his great Friend.

Some months passed and the parents of the students in the class continued their protests. Nonetheless, Jorgito didn't complain. The assignments continued to challenge him a lot, but he didn't complain about his poor grades. He simply dedicated more time to them.

One afternoon, Mamá realized that Jorgito approached the refrigerator and hung a worksheet on the door. It had been years since she'd seen him do this. Her curiosity was killing her, and so she proceeded to look at the paper. It was an English worksheet. It asked the students to list three high-risk professions.

Mamá was surprised with Jorgito's answer: "English student." His response had been circled in red by the teacher; and, in addition, written in capital letters there was a comment that read as follows:

LEARNING STANDARD:
Understands reality and interprets it with a
critical sense.
ACHIEVED WITH EXCELLENCE!
Final grade: B+

Mamá looked at her son and discovered a giant smile on his face that was almost too big for him. He was, without a doubt, satisfied with his work.

"Good work, Son!"

"Thanks, Mamá, but the next time it will be an A+. You'll see."

Chapter Eleven

JORGITO AND THE VALUE OF THE LITTLE THINGS[*]

And whoever gives only a cup of cold water to one of these little ones to drink because he is a disciple—amen, I say to you, he will surely not lose his reward.

MATTHEW 10:42

A LARGE family is a school of sanctity. And if not, then don't tell Jorgito. On Monday he woke up a little "cross" because his little sister had been taking his place at the table for several days.

To avoid unending arguments, it had been months since Papá had assigned seats in the dining room. He made the rules very clear: no one could change seats unless another member of the family agreed. His sister, who is very smart, spent days planning to test Jorgito's patience. She sat in his seat without asking permission, taking advantage of his struggle for holiness. Jorgito saw her, armed himself with patience, and, without saying a thing, sat in the chair that she left open. One day, two days, three days...

The Devil doesn't waste a single opportunity. And as we know, if there's anything that bothers him, it's finding a boy who wants to be holy. Because of this, he didn't stop whispering in his ear that his sister was an "opportunist." In the beginning, our boy struggled a lot not to listen, but in the end...

[*]Story first published in *Adelante la Fe* on January 30, 2015.

Jorgito came to the dining room angry. He imagined her in his seat looking at him mischievously with mocking eyes (the Devil knew how to do his work very well). And indeed, she was like that when he set foot in the dining room. Our boy couldn't take it anymore. He approached his sister and, without saying a word, gave her a little push on the shoulder.

The "bad luck" was that at the same time his sister was balancing the chair on its hind legs. Because of this, the chair gave out and his sister hit the ground, spilling the glass of milk that was in her hands all over her dress. What a disaster!

Mamá, who was in the kitchen, was alerted by the deafening scream that the girl let out. When she arrived, she found quite a scene: the girl completely stained, a puddle of milk (which the baby scattered happily across the entire floor of the dining room), Jorgito crying because of the disaster, the older brother laughing at what was going to happen to the boy... and only thirty minutes until it was time to go to school!

She was about to get angry but, nonetheless, without saying a word, returned to the kitchen. She took out a small holy card of Saint Martha and asked for help (this is something that Father Alfonso told her to do before he left for his new assignment. Saint Martha always helps housewives). She breathed deeply and went to the dining room again. But it was too quickly! So, she had to repeat this same thing twice more before the Saint intervened to give her patience:

"What has happened here?" she asked, looking at Jorgito (his scared face betrayed him).

Jorgito, crying, explained what happened. Mamá decided then and there to divide the housework. She made the older brother clean the floor (for laughing), she told the little girl to change clothes, and she decided to speak with her younger son in his room.

"Jorgito, I am going to give you a new friend," Mamá said as she handed him a small book. "Do you know Saint Dominic Savio?"

Jorgito shook his head, as he couldn't force himself to speak.

"Dominic Savio was a boy who wanted to be holy, like you. On the day he received his First Communion he wrote: "Die rather than sin." The boy stopped crying. Mamá had gotten his attention. "He wanted to do great things for Jesus, and he began to do penance. Some were not very appropriate for his age. When Saint John Bosco found out, he forbade him from continuing on with them. Do you know why?"

Again, he shook his head.

"Because Don Bosco taught him that holiness is not in the big things, but in the little ones. The first day that you gave your seat to your sister, the Lord was very happy. You were generous. But even more the second, the third... Do you know why? Because perseverance is the most valuable thing, Jorgito. It costs more. The Devil did not tempt you the first day because he knew that you wouldn't fall... But he is very clever, and he waited. The heroism of the first day was not enough incentive to give the seat to your sister again on the second day. Because of this, you were easy prey. Do you understand?"

Jorgito thought about it... and was amazed. The Christian struggle is so difficult! Mamá, satisfied by the intelligent silence of her son, left him alone with his book. Still, she had two talks pending with her other kids.

As is logical, they all arrived late to school. Jorgito had to explain himself to the teacher. Mamá told him that it was his responsibility. In the afternoon, the boy asked his father to take him to church for confession. His older brother did the same. They wanted to get rid of their sin as soon as possible. Father Antonio heard them individually in his office, rejoicing that he did not have more parishioners as scrupulous as this family. "If they were all like this, I could not leave my office," he said to himself, relieved.

Jorgito, alien to these thoughts, returned home wanting the night to arrive. He knew that his new friend Saint Dominic Savio would be waiting for him. And he wanted to ask him many things. That night our boy went to sleep very late.

The following morning, Jorgito was prepared to find his sister in his chair. He had resigned himself to sitting in her chair permanently. "The struggle is in the little things," he said. To his great surprise, he saw that his seat was empty. His sister was drinking her milk in the chair across from him. As soon as he took his seat, the girl explained:

"I also speak with Jesus. Last night He explained what envy is to me. I'm very sorry, Jorgito!"

Our boy was thrilled and got up from his seat. He gave his sister a big hug. He was proud of her. The problem is that, when he turned back to his seat, he found his brother Guille (two years old) there. In a large family, he who does not run, flies!

It was a tense moment. The looks descended upon our protagonist... Silence.

Suddenly, Jorgito cracked a smile. This time the Devil did not achieve his goal. And there is nothing that hurts him more than the smile of a boy who wants to be holy. His new friend Dominic had taught him that a good attitude is very important. And, no one said that the struggle was going to be easy!

Chapter Twelve

JORGITO AND THE GLOBALIZATION OF INDIFFERENCE*

Blessed are the poor in spirit, for theirs is the kingdom of heaven. Blessed are they who mourn, for they will be comforted.

MATTHEW 5:3-4

JORGITO's parish is in an uproar because of the 24 hour initiative for the Lord, proposed by the Holy Father in his Lenten address. Father Antonio called a meeting of the pastoral council to coordinate advertisement for the event, the organization of shifts, and background music to help prevent boredom. The priest had preached many homilies dissecting the Pope's Lenten address, excited as he was about the "globalization of indifference." So much so that he had proposed to end it in his parish. But of course! Because of this, he had made a point to increase donations of food for charity, much needed in this time of crisis.

Ignoring all of this racket, Jorgito's mom, who had a feeling while praying the Holy Rosary, decided to call Isabel who had been diagnosed with lung cancer just a few months ago. In the beginning, Isabel was surrounded by support: phone calls, encouragement, babysitters for her kids while she was undergoing chemotherapy treatments. But, as the cancer advanced (and hope receded), people began to make excuses:

"How can you comfort her?" "Poor woman; I can't stand to see her suffer." "I don't want to remember her like this." "It's so hard."

*Story first published in *Adelante la Fe* on February 14, 2015.

And so, Isabel felt the loneliness of her illness in the way that only a terminally ill patient can.

Jorgito, without meaning to, was the one who alerted his mom when he said that Juan, Isabel's son, wasn't going to his friends' houses. The moms argued about whether to invite him, because then they would have to bring their children to his house. And of course, no one wanted to risk their children seeing Isabel in this state.

Mamá, who did not usually allow friends to come over to the house (for simple, practical considerations: there wasn't much room, and if they started running there was the risk that, if someone sneezed, they'd fly out the window), decided to invite the boy over.

After a nice visit, they took him home. Juan's father thought that it was strange that Mamá asked to see Isabel. It had been so long since she had received a visitor! But he decided that Isabel would welcome the distraction. The ill woman got up with difficulty to receive her, thankful for the visitor. Jorgito, though he was struck by how ill she looked, greeted her courteously. He knew that she was very sick; they prayed for her when they said the rosary. On the other hand, Juan was happy to have a friend in the house and led Jorgito to his room. It was so wonderful to have company again!

Following that meeting, a friendship between the two woman arose. Mamá went to see her whenever she could and brought Jorgito with her. Juan needed a friend more than ever.

Soon Mamá discovered that the woman was a Catholic, but wasn't practicing. The last time she walked into a church was when her youngest son was baptized. She had not returned since. Her husband was an atheist. Because of this, the terrible illness (and the approaching outcome) had proven to be an unbearable yoke to carry. Knowing that she was going to leave her sons orphans and her husband a widower was an added burden to her suffering.

The first visits that Mamá made were spent simply listening to the sick woman. She listened to her worries, her fears, her sufferings... all until that one afternoon when Mamá interrupted to talk to her about God, death, and heaven. Isabel listened with a combination of attention, sadness, denial, and interest. It's so easy to speak about these things when you're healthy! But Mamá continued on and Isabel, each time, showed more interest. Sometimes Mamá was even able to sneak in a prayer. Other times, when Isabel struggled to maintain her breathing, Mamá prayed the rosary aloud while a silent tear escaped from Isabel's eyes.

"Don't fall into despair, Isabel. Put everything in God's hands and believe that, where you are going, you can intercede for your family." Isabel wept a tear, but without the bitterness of the first days. Her husband did not share these "ideas," but he let Mamá return because she brought peace to his wife.

As the result of a hunch, while praying the rosary, Mamá called her friend's cell phone. It wasn't she, but her husband who answered. Isabel was in the hospital. She wouldn't last long. Mamá asked permission to send a priest to give her the Anointing of the Sick. There was a long silence, but her husband agreed: he would respect his wife's beliefs.

Jorgito's mom no more than hung up when she called the parish. No one answered the phone, so she left a message on the answering machine. But she remained uneasy and began to pray to Padre Pio so that Father Antonio would get the message. Some time passed before her husband arrived home. Without allowing any time for greeting the kids, she asked him to go to the parish quickly to be sure that Father Antonio had given her the sacrament.

Jorgito's dad went to Father Antonio's office and found him busy looking at the computer screen.

"Excuse me, Father Antonio. Did you receive my wife's message?"

Father Antonio raised his head and said, "Ah, yes, the sick woman. Isabel, no? I haven't gone yet. I have been busy with meetings. When I'm finished, I'll go to the hospital."

As we have seen on another occasion, Jorgito's father is a real lion. And that day, Father Antonio saw it in person. Words were futile. The look on his face was enough for the priest to understand the error of his ways. Ashamed, he rose quickly and took his coat.

"I'm going right now."

An hour later, Jorgito's mom received a message on her phone. Isabel had died. Father Antonio had made it in time. Isabel had miraculously held on to life until Father Antonio administered the sacrament.

The funeral Mass, celebrated at the funeral home, was filled with relatives, friends, and parishioners. Everyone was crying at the tragedy. No children were there except Jorgito and his older brother, who had asked to accompany Juan. In the homily, Father Antonio praised Isabel's motherhood, her good deeds, how she had impacted the hearts of all those around her. He also assured them that she was already resting in heaven, after such a terrible illness. Thanks be to God, she had died in the state of grace.

Jorgito, meanwhile, asked himself how Father Antonio could know this; he had never spoken with Isabel. He also wondered how he knew that she was in heaven. His parents always prayed for the souls in Purgatory; and so, just in case, he took the opportunity to offer this Holy Mass for her. Jorgito was very conscious of the necessity to pray for souls.

At the end of the Mass, the parishioners returned to the church. That afternoon they had an appointment to gather the collection of food for charity. It was a complete success. They collected hundreds of pounds and Father Antonio could not have been more proud. The globalization of indifference? Not in his parish!

Chapter Thirteen

JORGITO AND LENT[*]

*The scribe said to him, "Well said, teacher. You are right in
saying, 'He is One and there is no other than he.' And 'to love
him with all your heart, with all your understanding, with all
your strength, and to love your neighbor as yourself' is worth
more than all burnt offerings and sacrifices."*

MARK 22:32-34

Jorgito's Lent did not go well. Our protagonist (who is
small, but not stupid) realized that something was wrong.
Every day that passed, he noticed that he was colder, with
more hardness in his heart; he was easily angered and dis-
tracted. If that wasn't enough, his great Friend, Jesus, did not
appear in prayer at night, and although he looked for Him,
Jorgito ended up sleeping in the dark loneliness of his room.
The boy was worried.

He had been like that since Ash Wednesday. That day, he
went to Mass with his family; just like every year. But, this
time, he noticed the attitude of the rest of parishioners, and
especially the children who were in catechism classes. Ob-
ligated by Father Antonio to "put the ashes on," the Holy
Mass turned into a constant stream of young lectors, teasing smiles because of the terrible reading, and bored parents
shamelessly looking at their watches, hoping that the next
words they heard would be, "You can go in peace."

Jorgito grew very sad. So much so that during the noisy
Consecration, he promised the Lord to give Him a wonderful Lent. "I will do a lot of penance, Lord. I will not do

[*]Story first published in *Adelante la Fe* on February 20, 2015.

like my classmates in catechism class who live apart from you." Because of this, that night he decided to prepare a plan for Lent, one well thought out. He included prayer, fasting, alms-giving, and penance. When he finished, he felt very proud. He had everything! The problem was that he ended up so tired that he forgot to say goodnight to the Lord. His head hit the pillow, exhausted.

The following morning, he began his plan with enthusiasm. He got up early without hitting the snooze button (something that cost him a lot), prayed his morning prayers, ate everything quickly (avoiding the chocolate cookies that he loved so much), and struggled not to complain when his mom reminded him (as she did every day) to comb his hair. "Mamá can sometimes be a real pain!!" he thought, bothered.

At school he continued his plan. He tried hard to do his homework in class, was determined to maintain his posture in his chair (it was so difficult to sit correctly!), offered to wipe the chalkboard... Jorgito felt very good. "Jesus must be happy," he thought every time he achieved his plan. And so the days passed... Our protagonist, who has a lot of willpower, fulfilled his plan to the letter. Nonetheless, as Lent progressed, he became increasingly sad. He didn't know exactly what was happening (it was difficult to explain), but Jorgito had so often been close to the Lord that he knew when he was far away from Him.

One afternoon, after school, Jorgito's mom put a homemade dessert on the table. The local grocery store had a sale on eggs, and since there were already so many in the refrigerator, Mamá decided to make lemon pudding for her children. Her oldest son, as soon as he saw it, asked permission to have some. "It tastes great, Mamá!" he said, licking his lips.

Jorgito lamented that his brother was not observing Lent as intensely as he was. That night, the boy again went to call upon the Lord, but silence was the response. This time our protagonist could not help but cry.

"Where are you, Lord?" he pleaded between sobs.

In answer to his sincere prayer, a new visitor appeared. He had a majestic and serious demeanor. He identified himself as Saint Jerome.

"Hello, Jorgito. The Lord sent me to you today. I want to tell you a story."

The boy opened his eyes attentively, for like all children, he loved stories.

"One Christmas the infant Jesus appeared to me and asked: 'Jerome, what are you going to give me for my birthday?' Touched, I responded, 'Lord, I give you my health, my reputation, and my honor, all to do with as you see fit.' But the infant Jesus did not seem pleased and added, 'And you won't give me anything more?' 'Oh, my beloved Savior!' I exclaimed. 'I have already given you all my possessions for the poor. I have dedicated my time to study the Sacred Scriptures for you... what more can I give you? If you want, I will give you my body to be burned at the stake so that my ashes will rise to surround you.'"

Jorgito understood Saint Jerome; in a certain way, he had also offered everything that he possessed. The saint continued the story:

"The Divine Child told me: 'Jerome, give me your sins so that I can forgive them.'"

The boy stared at the saint. He remained silent.

"Jorgito, what God wants most is for us to offer Him our sins with a humble and contrite heart, that we ask forgiveness for all of the sins that we've committed. Let me show you a scene from your life... not very long ago. Maybe you'll remember it."

Saint Jerome showed him what happened during dinner. There he was, refusing the pudding that his mom made. He was very frightened to see that there was a dark figure next to him, whispering things in his ear. In contrast, on the other side of the table was his older brother asking to have the dessert that Jorgito had refused. At his side was his guardian angel who looked pleased.

"I don't understand," Jorgito murmured.

"Look again. Notice your brother. His belly really hurt because breakfast didn't agree with him; he didn't feel well afterwards. But he realized that your mom had worked hard preparing that dessert. Because of this, as an act of love, he took your dessert too. He wanted your mom to feel appreciated. Now, take a look at yourself. You wanted God to see how good you were. You weren't doing it out of love, but out of pride. Because of this, you didn't realize your mother's hard work... nor your brother's. Be careful, Jorgito; pride is the easiest sin to cover up. The Devil knows it and takes advantage of it.

"Then, should I abandon my Lenten plan?" he asked Saint Jerome, worried.

"No, Jorgito. Review it again, but this time, let love guide it. Then, talk about it with the Lord. He will give you some ideas, too."

Jorgito did what the great Saint suggested. The following morning, he got up promptly. But this time, he ran to the bathroom to pick up the bathroom rug. During the past few days, he noticed that his older brother got up barefoot from the bed and went to the bathroom without any shoes on. The floor was very cold. He suspected that, since he had a hard time getting up, he was making a Lenten effort to overcome his laziness. Because of this, he placed it with love in the spot where his brother put his feet. He thought that he would appreciate finding a rug rather than a frozen marble tile that morning.

Then, during breakfast, without drawing any attention, he went to the kitchen to check on their school lunches. He saw that Mamá had prepared two sandwiches: one was made of ham, the other of cheese. Mamá had given him the ham and gave the cheese to his sister. He decided to change the sandwiches. His sister didn't like cheese very much... well, to tell the truth, neither did he. But he offered this sacrifice out of love.

When he left the house, he remembered to ask Jesus to be with him during the day. "Lord, give me a humble heart," he asked.

At recess, Jorgito reached into his backpack. He took the sandwich and opened it. He was surprised to find it was a ham sandwich. Didn't he switch with his sister? Confused, he looked up and caught his sister's eye, piercing him with a sweet look. In her hands was a half-eaten cheese sandwich.

It was then that he realized that his sister also spoke with Jesus every night. From what he could see, she had surpassed him with her Lenten plan. Love, together with prayer and penance, proved to be unstoppable.

Chapter Fourteen

JORGITO AND THE VIRTUE OF POVERTY

"Lord, when did we see you hungry and feed you, or thirsty and give you drink? When did we see you a stranger and welcome you, or naked and clothe you? When did we see you ill or in prison, and visit you?" And the king will say to them in reply, "Amen, I say to you, whatever you did for one of these least brothers of mine, you did for me."

MATTHEW 25:37-40

I T was a stormy night and Jorgito enjoyed watching the raindrops fall onto the asphalt of the city streets. As they bounced off the pavement the drops performed a synchronized dance which seemed magical to the boy. He loved the smell of the rain, most of all during Spring. He wanted so much to be at his country house!

Suddenly through the window pane, Jorgito fixed his eyes on the silhouette of a man who walked with difficulty. His clothes were completely wet and he pushed a shopping cart, which was missing its front wheel, just so that he could stay on his feet. The man took some steps and, after avoiding a huge puddle, stopped at the bank.

Intrigued by the man's behavior, the boy decided to study his movements. The stranger seemed to be expecting some- one and, despite the rain that continued to soak his body, remained at the entrance. What was he doing?

The storm lit up the sky and, all of a sudden, like a clap of thunder, a person holding a large umbrella approached from behind. "It must be the person he has been waiting for," thought the boy. But the newcomer ignored the stranger's presence and walked toward the door. Jorgito concluded that he must be a customer and continued looking out the window.

This time, Jorgito's guess was right: the man stood under the umbrella and took his credit card out to unlock the security system. However, something made him change his mind at the last minute. Jorgito noticed then that the stranger instinctively left some room between himself and the cart, which was on the verge of sinking due to the broken wheel, and only then did the man decide to enter.

Already at the ATM, the customer looked very nervous and pressed the buttons too quickly; he even pushed the wrong key twice. In the end, the machine vended some bills that the man quickly hid in his wallet. Much relieved, he made his way toward the exit and, when he began to leave, the stranger blocked the door with his cart. The customer, embarrassed and ashamed, fled from that place without looking back.

The boy continued watching, each time more interested. The cart's owner took a filthy blanket and covered the ground. Then, he left the ATM and rummaged through the trash, finding some cardboard which he used as an improvised bed.

Jorgito's heart began to pound in his chest; he had finally understood the scene: the ATM had become a bedroom.

"Mamá, Mamá!" Jorgito ran to the kitchen, where Mamá was preparing dinner for her husband. "Come quickly!"

"What's wrong, Son?"

"There is a man at the ATM! He is wet and doesn't have anywhere to sleep!"

Mamá approached the window and, indeed, she discovered a person sleeping under a blanket.

"What is he doing there?" the boy asked.

Jorgito was used to seeing beggars in the city. There were always two or three hoping for charity in the doors of the churches and in the streets too. But he imagined that they went home to sleep later. He never realized that they were homeless!

"He has taken refuge from the rain," Mamá began to explain. "There are poor people who don't want to go to the shelters and when it is cold or raining, they need to look for somewhere safe to sleep."

Jorgito, glued to the window now cold from the dampness, continued watching the beggar for some time.

"He is wet, Mamá..."

Mamá also watched him in silence. Finally, she decided to speak:

"Let's do this: as soon as Papá arrives, we'll go and take the man a hot meal."

Jorgito was overcome with emotion and went to the kitchen to prepare some delicious food. He was used to giving money to the poor after Mass, but he had never given food before.

"What do you think he would like?"

Mamá shrugged and looked in the refrigerator. Finally, she decided to prepare a cheese omelette and a bowl of fresh fruit. Jorgito announced that he would help with the preparations. Just as they finished, Papá walked in the door.

"Papá, Papá! You get to be the waiter!" announced Jorgito.

Papá looked to his wife for an explanation, and Mamá gave one. Papá was cautious at first, but he finally agreed to the proposal. He made a sandwich with the omelette, folding it and placing it inside of an English muffin, and put everything carefully inside a bag. Then, he opened the door and left.

Jorgito ran to the living room window like a shot, where he observed his father open the ATM and speak with the poor man for a moment. The stranger seemed to doubt for a moment, but nonetheless, extended his hand and received the bag that Papá offered.

The boy's heart was overflowing. The man had accepted the meal! When Papá came through the door Jorgito had so many questions:

"What did he say to you? Why didn't he go to a shelter? What's his name?..."

This time it was Papá who shrugged. He didn't talk to the man. He simply offered the food and left. Jorgito looked at him strangely.

"Papá, you always say that it is poor upbringing not to speak with others. Didn't you even ask his name?"

Mamá came to the rescue and told Jorgito that it was time for bed.

"It's very late," she reminded him, "and Papá hasn't had dinner."

While she tucked him in, Mamá decided to have a talk with her son:

"Jorgito, I once read that it is very difficult to treat a poor man with dignity. We think that the poor belong to us and we offer charity because it makes us feel good, but not because we are worried about them." The boy listened attentively and with a frown. "And so, when they don't react as we would like, we're sad."

"I don't understand, Mamá."

Mamá stroked his forehead.

"You know that Saint John of Avila brought food to the poor every night, and when he didn't have anything for them, they hit him!"

Jorgito's eyes got very big and he asked, "How is that possible?"

"Nonetheless, Saint John of Avila returned the next day with more love than the day before, if that's possible. Do you know why?" The boy shook his head. "Because the Saint saw Jesus in every poor person. He knew that what he was doing for them, he was doing for Jesus. So this is how they should be treated. Today you have reminded us that we should give them the same respect as we would give to anyone."

"Mamá is right," Papá interjected as he had heard the conversation from the hall. "I didn't behave very well with that man. I'm sorry."

The parents kissed their son and went to sleep. Jorgito remained deep in thought and decided to speak to his great Friend. He had many things to talk about. The following morning he woke up happy; he'd had a very intimate conversation with the Lord. On the way to school, he looked toward the ATM and noticed that the cart remained parked some feet away. Quickly he located the stranger sitting near a piece of old cardboard.

"Look, Papá, the man is still there."

Papá saw him and began to approach the beggar.

"Good morning, sir," Papá said as he extended his hand. "Last night I forgot to introduce myself. My name is Jorge and these are my children."

The man seemed surprised, but his face softened when he saw the smiling children's faces.

"My name is Francisco, and it's nice to meet you."

That laid the foundation for friendship between the homeless man and the family. The parents brought him dinner at night and the kids brought drawings in the morning. For some time all was well, but then...

Jorgito had been lying in bed for a while trying to fall asleep, but now he couldn't because Jesus was telling him very interesting things about heaven. Suddenly, he heard some shouting in the street. Someone was very mad. The shouting got louder and was becoming a disturbance, so much so that the boy was frightened and got out of bed to look out the window.

Francisco was outside, fighting against an invisible enemy. He was also shouting at pedestrians, who were running away scared.

"What's wrong with him?" Jorgito asked, worried. Almost ready to call his parents, the boy fell silent. Francisco had just slammed his cart into the glass of the ATM. The sound of the bank alarm was the only thing that silenced his shouting.

The police didn't waste any time in getting there and Jorgito saw how they took him. The tears streamed down his face. "Why? Why?" he asked again and again.

After a while, the boy felt a big hug. Mamá had come from her room, knowing how her son would be feeling.

"I am very sorry that you saw that, my dear."

"Why, Mamá? Why did he do that?"

There are times when adults don't have the answers; and in these cases, silence is the only thing that they can offer. Mother and son both held each other for a long while.

"Do you remember Saint John of Avila?" Mamá finally asked. "I think that tonight you should decide if you will return to treating Francisco with more love than before or if, on the other hand, you will be angry at him forever."

Jorgito remained silent and lay down on his bed. He didn't say a thing. The days passed and Francisco never appeared in the neighborhood again. Jorgito asked himself where he could be, as he had decided to forgive him. He wanted to see Jesus in his person, like Saint John of Avila had done.

One Sunday after Mass, the boy left the church with his mother. They were in the midst of an entertaining conversation when suddenly a smelly woman stopped Mamá and asked her for some money. She was so rude that Mamá felt badly about her request.

"I'm sorry, I don't have anything." she said plainly and continued walking.

When she finished speaking with her son, Mamá looked toward the woman, who continued begging in the door of the church. She didn't seem to be having much success, as her paper cup was empty. Mamá gave it a second thought and approached her.

"Take this, ma'am. Here is some money for you."

The woman waited for Mamá to drop the money in her cup and then sneered:

"And you said that you didn't have anything..."

Mamá's heart sank and Jorgito noticed immediately. Mamá clenched her fist to help control her emotions. Finally, relaxing, she shot him a smile:

"Jorgito, the poor are not ours, right?"

And the boy, understanding what she'd said, smiled.

"No, Mamá, no. They are not."

Chapter Fifteen

JORGITO AND THE FAMILY THAT OVERTOOK CHRIST[*]

Love is sufficient of itself, it gives pleasure by itself and because of itself. It is its own merit, its own reward. Love looks for no cause outside itself, no effect beyond itself. Its profit lies in its practice. I love because I love, I love that I may love.

SAINT BERNARD

J ORGITO was nearly asleep in his bed when he felt a sudden thirst. Deciding to fix that, he took a quick look at his brothers (his parents, except in emergencies, didn't let them get up; otherwise, the hallway would be changed into a constant stream of children asking for water, needing to go to the bathroom, and other similar excuses fully intending to avoid going to sleep); relieved, he noticed that they were all asleep. So, he quietly got out of the bunk bed and walked toward the kitchen. When he entered the living room, he discovered Mamá sitting on the couch with a book in her hand.

"What are you doing, Mamá?" he asked curiously.

His mom looked up, surprised. Jorgito thought he saw a tear in her eyes.

"You startled me, Dear; I didn't hear you come in," she said. (Jorgito noticed her voice didn't reflect annoyance.) "I was taking advantage of these few minutes to read before your father arrives. I hardly have time during the day, so I try to

[*]Story first published in *Adelante la Fe* on March 3, 2015.

find a few free moments when I can to do my spiritual reading."

Encouraged by his mother's smile and above all for the privilege of participating in such a special, intimate moment, our protagonist ventured to ask another question:

"What are you reading?"

Mamá closed the volume and showed him the cover. Filled with curiosity, Jorgito looked at the title: *The Family That Overtook Christ* by the Trappist M. Raymond.

"It's the story of the great Saint Bernard; well, of his whole family to be exact," she clarified. "The first time I read it, I was fifteen years old, and from then on, I re-read it whenever I can. It brings back many memories."

The boy walked cautiously toward the sofa, knowing that it was way past his bedtime, and sat next to his mother. He wanted to know more about the book. Relieved, he realized that she had made a space next to her.

"What's special about it?"

"A lot," she responded thoughtfully. "A lot. This book is the instruction manual for my life, Jorgito. I think that God put it in my path and uses it to tell me very important things. It's strange because at that time I was an avid reader; devouring whatever fell into my hands. And now I can hardly remember any book that I read during that time. On the other hand, I perfectly remember the exact moment in which I read this book, the bedside stand in my room where I kept it, and how much it inspired me."

Jorgito was surprised by his mother's confession. He wanted to know more.

"But why is it so special?"

"It tells the story of a real family of soldiers, of soldiers for Christ. Saint Bernard, with his courage, carried his brothers to holiness. And not only them, but his parents too."

They boy's eyes became as big as saucers. A story about warriors! And on top of that, one for him alone. This doesn't happen very often in a large family, so it has to be taken advantage of.

He bombarded her with questions: "What weapons did they use to fight? In what war? How did they win?"

Mamá couldn't help but to smile.

"Jorgito, they weren't that type of warrior. They were soldiers for God, Cistercian monks. All of them! And they fought with weapons that were more powerful than any that exist in the world: prayer, charity, and penance."

"Oh," the boy said, unable to hide his disappointment.

"Ha, ha, ha! You made the same face that Bernard's brothers did when they heard his proposal. You know? The first time that he told them about the monastic life, they were at the fortress of Grancy. I don't know if I told you, but his brothers were noble soldiers that fought in the service of their lord. They had earned well-deserved fame as brave soldiers, skilled in the use of arms. But then, one day, during the war, Bernard appeared and told them about the possibility of being generous men, heroes, who gave everything to God, being at His knightly service." The boy became more interested. "How wonderfully he must have spoken to them, Jorgito, that one by one they abandoned their storybook lives to return to the the silent life of the monastery! Can you imagine it? He got thirty men to abandon their place at Grancy to go to Citeaux."

Jorgito wasn't convinced. He didn't understand why they had to renounce their heroic lives for God.

"Make no mistake, my son! The battle for holiness is the longest and most difficult of all. And this family fought like no other. They all struggled to overtake Christ. One by one, they were infected by Bernard's spirit, from the oldest brother Guy to the youngest brother Nivard; even his sister Humbeline, with all of her beauty, abandoned her noble life to join the Cistercian convent! All for the fight for God, for Christ. The result: six siblings who are Blessed and one Saint, the great Saint Bernard. And there's even one more monk to add to the family list. Do you know who?"

It was a question with an obvious response, and Jorgito was anxious to know it.

"The father, Jorgito! The father also went to Citeaux to spend the last years of his life there. And Tescelin was a great nobleman with a lot of influence!"

"He wanted to be with his children?"

"No, he wanted to give his life in better service of God. At the beginning he thought that, being an old man, he couldn't endure the hard life in the monastery. But Bernard asked him a question that dispelled all of his doubts: 'Can't you pray, Father?'" Mamá remained silent for a moment. "Jorgito, I admire this father more than any of his children."

"Why?" he asked fascinated.

"Because he knew how to submit himself, out of obedience and love of God, to his sons. Imagine that! A brave warrior, advisor to the duke and used to giving orders, suddenly abandoning everything and becoming a simple monk, subject to the rules of his kids: clean the stable, till the garden, clear the table... and he did it all without complaint! He did it for the glory of God. Isn't it incredible? And for this heroic feat, today the Order of Citeaux calls this old warrior Venerable.

Jorgito understood Mamá, but he had one doubt:

"And why," he wanted to know, "did this book change your life? You didn't become a monk like them."

"Ha, ha, ha! You are right, my son. It certainly wasn't because of that. To see the answer, tell me who is missing in this story."

Jorgito barely had to think before he replied, "the mother!"

"Yes, Alice of Montbar, or better, Blessed Alice of Montbar. The book changed my life because it was there that I discovered Alice, Jorgito. She was only 15 years old when she married Tescelin. She never thought that Jesus wanted this life for her, but on the contrary, she wanted to be a nun in the convent. Tescelin, however, dared to ask her father for her hand in marriage. And do you know what Alice's response was? She agreed because of the holy obedience that she had toward her father, knowing that the will of God was different from her own. Alice understood that the secret of holiness is found in simply doing the will of God with good will. She was convinced that Christ wanted her to be the wife of Tescelin and the mother of six children. And so she did exactly that, abandoning her laudable project in order to dedicate herself in body and soul to her family, to the life that God made for her."

Mamá looked at the book for a minute. "She had a goal, Jorgito: to bring the members of her family to holiness, and to do it with humility, without a great fuss or showy miracles. Son, part of the book's thesis is that a family of saints doesn't happen by accident. For the grace of God to be effective, it must fall on a fertile, well-prepared field. Alice planted the ground, both naturally and supernaturally at the same time. She schooled them in the virtues, teaching them to pray, to practice charity; and God responded abundantly, as always. Note that, in the end, she managed to send her whole family into the cloister! What she wanted for herself at first, she shared with her family! And in doing so, she did, with simplicity, the will of God."

Jorgito was amazed. He wanted to take the book out of his mother's hands.

"Can I read it?"

"Not yet, Son. You are too little to understand it in its entirety," Mamá said as she rose and placed the book on the shelf of the living room library. "But I will leave it here for when God tells you you're ready, when you can read it carefully. And now, to bed you little scoundrel! You have already lost too much sleep because of our talk."

Jorgito's intrigued look showed Mamá that, essentially, some day he would read this precious book. She tucked her son into bed again and returned to take a final look at the book that was resting in the library. Her husband should be home soon.

"Alice, care for my family. May God grant me the same simple wisdom that He gave you, so that I might bring the members of my family to holiness. I ask simply that, some day, I might present God with the same crown that you did: a family that overtook Christ."

And with this simple prayer, Mamá went to the kitchen to make dinner for her husband who was nearly home after a long day at work.

Chapter Sixteen

JORGITO AND THE STATIONS OF THE CROSS[*]

*Then Jesus said to his disciples, "Whoever wishes to come after
me must deny himself, take up his cross, and follow me."*

MATTHEW 16:24

Jorgito's family found themselves in their country house enjoying a Spring weekend. During the morning they worked in the small garden that the family decided to plant some months ago—it was so wonderful to pick the first green beans!—and they spent the afternoon running around the property in search of the chocolate coins that Grandma had given them. It took them some time to make a treasure map, but the search that followed through the trees, the bushes, and the boulders was worth it.

Enjoying the vivid sunset, Papá, inspired by the beautiful day, decided to celebrate a family *Via Crucis*.

"Kids, I need two pieces of wood! We are going to make a cross!"

"Why, Papá?" asked the curious oldest brother.

"You'll see."

The children began their search, and in less time than it took to devour the chocolates, they appeared triumphantly with two small pieces of wood in their hands. Papá used a piece of wire that he had inside the house to join the wood and, in this way, produced a humble yet noble cross.

---

[*]Story first published in *Adelante la Fe* on March 11, 2015.

"It will work well. Now, come and sit closer as I tell you what we're going to do. Do you know what the *Via Crucis* is?"

"Yes," responded Jorgito. "It is what we did last year when we painted the pictures of Jesus and put them all over the house!"

His parents smiled and exchanged a knowing glance. Apparently, the effort spent coloring all of the stations with their children bore fruit; the older children remembered the years past.

"That's it! Last year we celebrated a *Via Crucis* in the house. This year, what if we do one in the mountains?"

"Yes!!" they responded excitedly, though without knowing exactly what this '*Via Crucis*' meant.

"Excellent!"

Papá thought for a moment before explaining. "In Latin, *Via Crucis* means 'The Way of the Cross.' Jesus walked a long way to Mount Calvary where he was crucified. The *Via Crucis* attempts, through fourteen stations, to accompany Our Lord during this difficult time. It's important that you pay attention, because if the stations are legitimately erected, you can obtain a plenary indulgence. Unfortunately, we don't have them here, but we can also obtain graces. To do that, we will read a short meditation at each station to enter into the mystery of the Passion. Then, we will walk a while to the next station, singing a verse of the *Stabat Mater Dolorosa*. We'll each take our turn, from the oldest to the youngest, carrying the cross (except Jaime who is too little); and we'll carry it with respect, with piety, and raised high. If we do it well, we can unite ourselves to Jesus Christ who climbed the hill of Calvary. What do you think?"

This time, the "yes" was not as cheerful as before. The children had grasped the gravity of what they were about to do, so they were more reflective and acted decisively. They all gathered around Papá, who elevated the cross reverently.

Mamá opened a little book that she kept in her missal and read it in a loud voice:

"The first station: Jesus is condemned to death. We adore you, O Christ, and we bless you."

"Because by your holy Cross you have redeemed the world," Papá responded.

"Jesus had done nothing wrong, for He did all things well. He went about doing good to others, curing the sick, expelling demons, pardoning sinners, but He was condemned to death. There are things that we cannot understand, but Jesus completely accepted the will of the Father, being obedient unto death and death on a cross." She paused for a few seconds to meditate upon what had been read, and then continued. "We must also be obedient to our parents, although sometimes we don't understand the reasons. It is not about staying out of trouble, but about showing God that we love imitating His life of obedience. Our Father..."

Walking toward the second station, Jorgito thought about obedience. It was so hard and cost so much! Above all, those times when his parents unjustly told him to share a toy with his sister that always ended up broken or to set the table the day it wasn't his turn. But Jesus was obedient, and His death was a true injustice. "Then, what little right I have to complain!" he thought to himself. He looked at the cross, which Mamá was now carrying, and resolved to better accept these inconvenient orders. Meanwhile, the family continued their song (off-key, but with no less devotion) to the second station where this time Papá read:

"The second station. Jesus carries the Cross. We adore you, O Christ, and we bless you."

"Because by your holy Cross you have redeemed the world," replied Mamá with the oldest children joining her in chorus, as they'd learned the response quickly.

"Jesus had to carry a heavy cross and we can imagine that He was tired after they crowned Him with thorns and scourged Him, but He carried the cross. He made this sacrifice for us. He showed us what the virtue of fortitude really is." They paused in silence. "We also have to suffer by studying when we don't want to. It's a sacrifice that we should do very well, because then we can offer it to Jesus as a job well done, trying to please Him, not leaving assignments until the last minute or doing them quickly or poorly. Bearing the weight of our cross with joy, we take a bit of the weight of His cross from Jesus. Our Father..."

And so they went from station to station, alternating between carrying the cross and singing songs of penance and praise. Every member of the family meditated on the Passion of Christ and determined to apply it to his own life. When little Guille took it, he carried the cross skillfully, his steps forming a kind of zigzag due to the weight of the cross. It's almost bigger than he is! Nevertheless, he refused to accept Papá's help and strayed off the path, as if saying, in his own way, that this was his cross.

From the seventh station on, the littlest ones began to get tired and impatient, but Mamá and Papá tried to skirt their interruptions with more or less patience. "What are these discomforts when compared with yours, Lord?" Mamá said while giving Jaime the pacifier for the hundredth time. When they arrived at the twelfth, Papá announced the station with devotion, "Jesus dies on the cross." He looked at his family and said: "kneel for a moment."

Heaven rejoiced because at that moment Jaime, the baby, stopped crying having noticed a butterfly fly near him. And, although his silence didn't last long (otherwise it would have been a miracle), it was sufficient to savor the moment. After a few seconds had passed, the head of the family rose and continued with the reading:

"Jesus died for us sinners, giving us the opportunity for salvation. Because of this, when we approach the Sacrament of Confession, the fact that our sins are erased might seem simple to us, but only because He first paid for all of them. Let us frequently approach the Sacrament of Confession that our souls might be washed clean, for then they are like Jesus' soul.

"Mamá, why did Jesus have to suffer so much?" the little sister asked.

"Because love is exaggerated, my dear; if not, it is not love. Our Father..."

Jorgito deeply meditated on each station. Each one said something distinct, reminded him of something that he could improve, or prompted him to give thanks to God for all that he had received. Because of this, when the time to begin walking to the last station had arrived, he asked his mother whether he might please be able to carry the cross. He wanted to carry it, like Simon of Cyrene, to Calvary; he wanted to accompany Jesus to the end. Mamá saw such resolve on his face that she gave permission without hesitation. The climb to the last station coincided with the final rays of daylight. The cross looked resplendent, like an arrogant challenge to the horizon. Jorgito carried it with gracefulness, and the rest of the family followed with devotion. Mamá watched her son and, during this intimate moment, remembered her silent prayer to carry her family to Jesus Christ. On the other hand, Papá watched his little boy and could hardly control his deep uneasiness: the image of his son carrying the cross made him recall the day of his son's baptism.

"Jorgito, that day the priest first marked you with the sign of the cross, and we did the same, but how often we forget that we are bound to the same destiny as Christ!" Papá thought to himself. "You will walk gloriously to the resurrection, but first, my son, you will have to carry your own cross.

Will you remember to carry it the same way that you did to-day?" he said while watching, "or will you end up rejecting it?"

Then he thought about all the difficulties that life would bring him: frustrations, loss of loved ones, disappointments. While that frightened him, he was even more worried about the very crosses that his son would suffer for being a Christian: rejection, religious persecution from both outside and inside the Church, the misunderstanding of those closest to him, the temptations of Satan. He had had many conversations with Father Alfonso about this fact. And the priest always concluded that he should give his children an education of a "turtle shell," one that was able to teach them to retreat to safety while under attack and that, later, would serve to protect them from blows. "Because yes, your children will suffer. And the closer that you approach holiness, the greater your suffering will be."

He was about to falter, but then he clung tightly to his own cross, the one that comes from being a father, the one that was particularly his, and kept going. Jorgito, unaware of his father's anguish, looked with love at the cross that he was holding. "Lord, I don't want to leave you alone. Let me accompany you! Until the end! And all so that one day I can enjoy you in heaven."

Jorgito was surely not aware that Love, in addition to being exaggerated, is also accommodating. If he had known this, he would not have made his prayer with such courage. Or maybe he would have, because children are generous, and Jorgito, at his tender age, had already begun to know true Love.

"O Victory, you shall be king; O Cross, you save us..." resounded mightily between the mountains, whose echo returned the verse as if the whole of nature were proclaiming this great Truth. And in reality, so it was, because the verse was not only sung by the family, but also, in an inaudible way, by the Triumphant Church in heaven who accompanied the family on their ascent to Calvary.

Chapter Seventeen

JORGITO AND NATURE[*]

For some time the wolf went quiet
in the holy asylum.
Its vast ears heard the Psalms
and his clear eyes moist.
He learned many graces and made a thousand tricks
when going to the kitchen with the friars.
And when Francis prayed,
the poor wolf licked his sandals.

RUBÉN DARÍO

JORGITO's family planned a new mountain hike, but before starting the route they decided to stop in the village to buy a loaf of rustic bread. While his parents went into the bakery, the harsh voices of two hunters who were waiting at the door caught Jorgito's attention. They seemed to be celebrating something, so, like any child would do, he approached the trailer with curiosity.

"Good morning Boy! Want to see our trophy?"

Jorgito didn't hesitate a moment and looked inside: a huge boar, with menacing fangs, lay dead.

"Ha, ha, ha! Lad, this animal was eating acorns a few hours ago!" exclaimed the older hunter proudly.

Our protagonist could not take his eyes away from the animal. He had never suspected that the mountain housed such dangerous guests. Mamá and Papá approached the vehicle, and the hunters explained that they had caught their prize just five miles from the village.

[*]Story first published in *Adelante la Fe* on March 20, 2015.

81

"We saw a large herd, but we were only able to catch this one!" commented the youngest.

After a few minutes of small talk, the parents said good-bye and drove toward the starting point of their hike. Jorgito couldn't stop thinking about those wild boars and, when he came out of the vehicle, for the first time in his life he was afraid of the mountain.

The trek began with the invocation of Saint Joseph; the feast of this great saint—to whom Papá is very devoted—was approaching and the family was offering a novena. Therefore, although the hikes usually started with the Rosary, this time they decided to replace it with the corresponding meditation (Saint Joseph being Mary's husband, they believed that she wouldn't object):

"O most gracious Jesus, just as your beloved father travelled from Bethlehem to Egypt to get rid of the tyrant Herod, so we humbly pray, through the intercession of Saint Joseph, to free us from those who want to harm our souls and bodies, to give us strength and salvation in our persecutions, and in the midst of the exile of this life, protect us until we fly to the motherland," read Papá.

Jorgito clung to this request and asked Saint Joseph to protect them from wild animals. His imagination was running wild; he saw dangers everywhere. Papá soon realized something was wrong:

"What's the matter, Son?"

"I'm afraid of wild boars..."

Papá thought for a moment, stopped the march, and asked the family to sit around him.

"Do you want to know how Saint Francis tamed a terrible wolf? They say that it was so fierce that it devoured animals and men alike... The whole land was terrified and no one dared to leave the city. When they did, they were armed as if they went to war." That story wasn't helping our protagonist;

on the contrary, he was getting more nervous by the second. "Saint Francis, upon hearing the news, set out to meet the wolf, disregarding all warnings; and the only weapon he took with him: his trust in God. The animal, when it heard Saint Francis coming, approached him with his open jaws, but the Saint, making the sign of the cross, said defiantly: 'Come here, Brother Wolf! I command you, on behalf of Christ, not to hurt me or anyone.' The fierce animal, obedient to the cross, closed its mouth and went to him meek as a lamb. Saint Francis spoke to him and sealed a pact: the animal would be adopted by the town of Gubbio in exchange for not hurting anyone. And so, from that day, the wolf came into the houses to ask for food and the citizens opened their doors fondly. What does this story say to you?"

"That the saints do great miracles..." the older brother said, amazed by the story.

"True, but it's something more. It means that nature is at the service of God. The great saints understood this. Do you know that Saint Anthony of Padua, in a sermon, got the fish to listen to him? Therefore, my children, you must not be afraid of nature. Respect it, yes; for it is not ours, but God's. But do not be afraid of it; after all, it is God's gift to us." The head of the family looked at his son: "Jorgito, you can relax, boars do not go out during the day; They are nocturnal animals..."

"Papá," interrupted the boy, "the wolf went to heaven when it died?"

The child had been impressed by the story and thought the wolf had undergone a conversion.

"No, Son. Animals do not go to heaven."

Jorgito did not expect this answer.

"Why?" and his thoughts drifted to Duke; the old German Shepherd with whom they played in the early years of the cottage. It belonged to the neighbor, but eventually they ended up adopting it as their own. So when it died it was very painful for the children.

"Jorgito, Heaven means to contemplate the beautiful face of God. It is a reality reserved for angels and humans. We are endowed with immortal souls, and that privilege belongs to us."

"It's not fair. What happened to Duke, then?" he replied.

"Children, do animals go to school?" asked Papá looking to find ways to explain, to those who were so young, something so complex. "No, right? Why? Because they would not understand anything. They could spend years and years in the classroom, and it would be like the first day. Something similar happens with Heaven. I know it is a simplistic explanation, but it can serve as an example."

"Then, why did God create them?" insisted the elder brother, still unconvinced.

"The Lord also put Creation at the service of man. Duke fulfilled his function, nobly. He looked after us, he protected us, and we we responded with love. That's not bad; on the contrary. Don Bosco also had a guard dog, Grigio. He appeared out of nowhere one autumn night. At first the priest was afraid, because it was large. But since it was not aggressive, he approached it to pet it. After that, every time the saint was alone in a dangerous situation, that dog mysteriously emerged, and then faded. There are many stories told by the saint himself about how the dog saved him from very dangerous situations. The animal never accepted food but it loved being petted by Don Bosco and his children. When the persecutions stopped, Grigio disappeared. The Saint missed the animal very much."

The family listened spellbound.

"That's why, Children, is not bad to love animals. What we mustn't do is succumb to the temptation to grant them a dignity that not even God has given them. We can't do that."

This time, the children agreed more. And, on the other hand, they began to realize their own dignity. Mankind was made for heaven. This reality is taken so lightly!

The family continued the hike. Jorgito, still a little nervous and upset about it, decided to stay behind to overcome his fear. He had always felt comfortable in nature! Also, if Saint Francis had managed to tame a wolf, he would at least be able to trust God. "Nature is at the service of man," he said again and again.

The family disappeared around a curve and the child found himself alone, accompanied only by his imagination, which did not hesitate to play tricks on him. It took only a few seconds for the little child to hear a noise behind a bush. Frightened, he froze... until a harmless rabbit emerged from the bushes.

"Yikes!!" he sighed. With great relief he turned around, but this time he let out a huge scream that echoed through the mountains. Paying attention to the bushes, he had not noticed the huge figure that had quietly come up behind him.

"Jorgito! It's me, Papá! I saw you were behind and I came back to get you."

Completely embarrassed, the boy stuck his head between his father's legs.

"Son, do not be ashamed of your fear. Everyone is afraid of something. He who does not fear is either reckless or foolish. But you, nevertheless, have faced it. And therein lies true valor."

Jorgito reared his head from between his father's legs and looked into his eyes.

"You are afraid of things too, Papá?"

Papá smiled and nodded. The boy was shocked by this revelation and felt like he was just let in on a big secret. His father also afraid...

"Don't worry! I won't tell anybody!"

The man laughed out loud and Jorgito grabbed his hand affectionately. Now he walked along happily; the boars had been forgotten. Papá looked at him quietly and proudly. "Jorgito, a Christian must be brave. And today you have shown courage. If you go on like this, Son, someday, you'll be great," he thought to himself.

The rabbit looked at them and, had it been aware of what was happening, surely would have smiled at the scene; instead, the animal continued nibbling nervously on its branch, oblivious to the beauty of the moment.

Chapter Eighteen

JORGITO AND NEW TECHNOLOGIES[*]

"Martha, Martha, you are anxious and worried about many things. There is need of only one thing. Mary has chosen the better part and it will not be taken from her."

LUKE 10:41-42

"JORGITO, it's rude to interrupt a conversation," corrected Mamá while talking to her husband. "It's not polite." The child waited nervously for his turn; he found the waiting to be very long!

"Now, Honey. What did you want?"

Jorgito began to describe how eager he was to see the processions of Holy Week: the beating of the drums announcing the departure of the penitents overwhelmed him; he was amazed by the slow pace of the penitents; he was thrilled with the holy thrones...

"Wait, Son. I just remembered I have to ask grandma to hem your tunic."

Mamá picked up her phone and texted Grandma. Meanwhile, Jorgito, having been cut off, was confused about what Mamá had just done. "Wasn't it rude to interrupt?" he thought annoyed. However, he failed to make a comment, well advised by his guardian angel.

"Sorry, it was important. What were you saying?"

"Never mind, Mamá. It was nothing."

[*]Story first published in *Adelante la Fe* on March 28, 2015.

87

Jorgito went to school where the teacher asked what they would do during the holidays. The students got excited and exploded in choir.

"How many times have I told you: one by one! I can not handle two conversations at once!" criticized the teacher.

"As soon as I leave school on Friday I'm going to the beach with my family!" said a brimming voice from the back.

The teacher, startled, exclaimed: "Oh no! I forgot to tell your parents that school finishes on Friday at one o'clock! Hold on a second while I send a quick email..."

Again, the class waited impatiently until the teacher finished writing the email on her mobile. "Done. Now what were you telling me?"

In the afternoon, Father Antonio met with all the children of catechism class to explain the *Via Crucis* which would be held on Friday in the parish: "During the Stations of the Cross, Children, you have to be quiet and respectful. Do not talk, laugh, or whisper to the person next to you... One has to know how to behave. Understood?"

Jorgito was going to ask if it was possible to invite their classmates, but before he had the opportunity, the priest´s phone rang: "Yes? Oh, hi! No, it's fine; you're not interrupting anything important. Tell me, tell me..." shouted the priest while his finger ordered the children to remain silent.

"How rude!" thought the priest, annoyed at the noise caused by the children.

After the catechesis, Jorgito went to the park to play with his friends. While they were up on the slide, a mother, who until then had sat on the bench fiddling with her smartphone, approached them excitedly:

"My, how handsome you all look! I'll take a picture for my Facebook!"

Without asking permission, she took the photo and posted it online with the title: "An afternoon with my son." Having obtained her trophy, she returned to the bench and buried her head in her phone waiting for someone to comment. "The picture is so pretty that I'm sure I'll get many 'likes' among my friends," she thought, delighted. Jorgito looked at her and wondered what would have happened if they had taken a picture of her instead.

Finally it was time for dinner and the whole family sat around the table.

"Papá, can I finish watching the documentary on TV?" asked the elder brother.

"No, son. We enjoy dinner together as a family. We don't watch TV or take toys to the table," he reminded them while he waited patiently for Guille to deposit his toy car in the toy box.

Mamá left her phone on the edge of the table, which was a problem because, as could be expected in this new technological age, a video soon popped up on her phone. Mamá took a look and saw that her nephews were at home with Grandma; surely they had gone to visit her.

"Look how adorable! Wait a moment so that I can also shoot a video for Grandma..."

The daughter posed in front of the camera with astonishing ease; she was accustomed to the attention. She also liked it. Jorgito, however, couldn't stand it anymore:

"I don't want to, Mamá! Forgive me, but I'm sick of phones, pictures, videos...! I just want you, when you are with me, to be with me. No phones, or laptops, or tablets. If Jaime does something funny, just laugh, do not record it for posterity. If Guille cries, you do not need Papá to instantly find out by WhatsApp; instead, comfort him. If I talk to you, listen to me, even if your phone rings..."

Jorgito suddenly realized that he had caught the attention of the entire table and, ashamed, ran crying to his room. The whole family was silent, especially Mamá.

Papá adjourned the family meeting and nodded to his wife. It was time to talk and make decisions. The children, aware of the moment, cleared the table quietly without disturbing them. After a conversation in the bedroom, Mamá came to see Jorgito.

"I'm really sorry, Son. I was not aware of how badly I was acting." Jorgito, with his eyes red from crying, looked at his mother. "From now on, phones will only be used at home for incoming calls... and we will never interrupt a conversation because of them. We will look at our messages just before bed. If someone has something important to say, they will call again. As for the pictures or videos we will only record them on special occasions, with your permission. What do you think?"

The child, in response, gave his mother a big, emotional hug. It was so good to feel understood!

"And, Honey, if you ever notice that I fall again, please correct me. Do it with love and discretion, as we have taught you. Adults also need correction, even more than children..."

At night, Jorgito told the Lord about his day.

"Jesus, sometimes I think if you had a smartphone, you would reach more people. Adults spend the whole day in front of screens."

Jesus laughed at the comment and answered amused:

"Apparently, you're not the only one who thinks so. In fact, I'm tracking down a Twitter account; when I see that it wins a real conversion, I will think about it. Meanwhile, I'll stick with traditional methods as, in the end, they are the ones that get results."

Chapter Nineteen

JORGITO AND THE VIRTUE OF FORGIVENESS

Blessed are the merciful, for they shall obtain mercy.
MATTHEW 5:7

P APÁ was out with his two eldest sons. He liked taking walks with them, as he found that doing so opened up the stomach, preparing it in anticipation of Mama's home cooking, as well as the heart. That's why, whenever possible, he took his boys out with him.

"Papá, I do not understand the Parable of the Prodigal Son," said Jorgito just as they passed the corner market. "Well, I understand the story, but not the message. Why did the father throw a party upon his son's return? The son behaved very badly."

"You're right," answered the father. "The younger son didn't act well."

"Of course not!" interrupted Pablo, happy that, on this occasion, the eldest wasn't the bad guy. "He acted pretty vile. First, he left the house with his father´s money and then, when he had nothing left, he came back. And to top that, he found a party thrown in his honor!"

"Exactly!" Jorgito said. "That's unfair! It's like if you reward me for not doing homework, or for not cleaning my room or..."

"Not eating our vegetables!" exclaimed Pablo with conviction.

Papá listened attentively until they finished their arguments. For once, both sons agreed on something, so he seized the moment.

"Let's see, Children, there really is no easy answer. The younger brother made a decision and left home with his inheritance. Then, instead of using it sparingly, he squandered it."

"What does that mean?" asked an attentive Jorgito.

"To squander something means to waste it. The younger son misused his father's money and ended up losing everything. At first, one might expect the younger son to work hard to recover the money or that, upon his returning home, his father would impose a severe punishment..."

"Of course! He deserved it!" Pablo said righteously.

"But the father does not do that, he does something completely unexpected."

"A party, Papá!" complained Jorgito. "And not just party. A big party!"

Papá was silent for a moment. "Why do you think he did that?"

"Because parents always forgive their children," responded Pablo angrily; and Jorgito nodded in agreement. In a way, they felt let down. They expected a great punishment.

"I see that you feel like the elder brother of the story."

The children blushed at the comment. They knew that in the end the elder son didn't come out so well.

"Don't worry, we all have felt like that at some point in our lives. I'd be lying if I said otherwise. In a certain way, it would have been fair. But then, why do you think that the Lord left us this Parable?"

After spending some time thinking, they shrugged their shoulders.

"Let's think about the Parable again. Who does the father represent?"

"God!" they answered at the same time.

"Very good. The father of the Prodigal Son represents God. And how is God's love?"

"Immense," said Pablo.

"Infinite," responded Jorgito.

"I'd say incomprehensible," Papá declared. "God's love is incomprehensible to us. As much as we try, His love escapes us. Because His love... is free. It is a love that expects nothing in return; and human beings, without the grace of God, are not capable of loving this way."

"We can't?" they exclaimed in amazement.

"No. Human beings always seek one thing: to receive love. Instead, God doesn't demand it, He only waits for it. The Parable of the Prodigal Son is the way the Lord uses to explain that great truth."

"Then He will always forgive us? Whatever we do? That easily?" Jorgito asks, still not convinced."

"You tell me. Look at the Parable again slowly. Did the father bring the younger son back home?" The children shook their heads from side to side. "No, right? So what did the younger one do to win the party?"

"Nothing. He just returned," said Pablo.

"Pablo, think about whether it was easy to return home. Would you have gone back knowing that your big brother was ready to hold your sins against you? Or would you rather have stayed away so that he didn't discover your shame?"

This time he did not answer so quickly. He thought about his brother's laughter.

"I don't know..."

"And with what attitude did he return home? With demands? With new rights?"

"No, he came back sorry. He even wanted to become a servant," said Jorgito. Gradually their eyes were beginning to open. The Parable no longer seemed so unfair.

"What does the house represent in the Parable?"

"The Church!" responded Pablo joyfully. "It's the Church! I understand now, Papá. The younger brother went to church and repented of his sins."

The father nodded. "And upon returning, he found a loving father who, far from reproaching his faults, was only concerned only about restoring the dignity of his son. Isn't that wonderful?! God is great, remember it."

"But then, if God's love is incomprehensible, we can't love like He does?" asked Jorgito with curiosity. As a child, he was reluctant to set limits.

"I didn't say that. I said that it is incomprehensible, not that it is impossible. In fact, we are called to identify ourselves with Jesus Christ and therefore we must love as God does. But alone, we cannot. We can only do it with the help of grace."

They continued the walk talking about other things, but both brothers kept the conversation in their hearts. Days later, returning from school, they found an apocalyptic scene in their room. Guille, their younger brother, had climbed a chair in the morning and managed to grab a Lego starship they both had safely tucked away on the shelf.

Jorgito had worked weeks to finish the ship and was very proud of it. In fact, it was one of the few toys that he really had enjoyed playing with. Therefore, to see the parts spilled around the room like Humpty Dumpty was a terrible blow. Meanwhile Guille watched with horror, guilt, and fear; all at the same time. The ship was completely destroyed.

"What have you done?" cried Jorgito disconsolately. "It took me a lifetime to build. It was mine!"

Angry tears trickled down his cheeks. "Get out of here! I do not want to see you!" he yelled to his brother.

Guille ran crying from the room while Jorgito, in vain, tried to join the pieces he found on the floor.

"I'll help you," Pablo told him, realizing his brother's pain. "Maybe we can rebuild it."

The two brothers spent the afternoon locked in the room, but they could not undo the damage. Various parts were missing and the instructions were lost. The starship they put back together didn't look anything like the original.

During dinner, Jorgito didn't look at Guille. To say he was angry with him was an understatement. The small one seemed to have shrunk two feet, brought low under the weight of his guilt. During dinner hardly any words were said.

Then, bedtime came. How much Jorgito longed to share his pain! He was eager to tell his great Friend about the mess Guille made. He deserved a great punishment! Jesus heard him and when he finished He asked a question:

"Jorgito, you're right. Guille has done wrong. He picked up something that was not his and broke it. That is not right." The child heard, but surprisingly, wasn't happy about those remarks. He wasn't even relieved. Moreover, he began to worry. "Do you think he deserves a punishment?"

This time Jorgito thought harder. He was not used to having his Friend agree so easily.

"Well, he knew he could not touch it, but... he's small."

Jesus smiled at Jorgito's hesitation.

"Don't excuse him, Jorgito. Guille knew he was doing evil. Justice would be to punish him, right?" Jorgito nodded silently. "Then, Jorgito, whenever man sins does he deserve a punishment?"

The child meditated in silence. Those were harsh words.

"I suppose so, Lord."

"And against an infinite evil as sin, what punishment must be imposed? One small, big...?"

"One proportionate."

"Exactly! And then, why don't men suffer that proportionate punishment?"

The boy did not know the answer until Jesus showed him His wounds. "Jorgito, I offered myself for you; I died on the cross to save mankind. A sacrifice of infinite value for an evil of infinite offense. But, just like the Prodigal Son, man has to accept it. God can not draw men back to the Church. It is man who, in his freedom, must return."

Our protagonist listened spellbound. So many things yet to learn! Freedom, love, gratitude, sacrifice... too much for such a small mind.

"Lord, you love us too much," said a sleepy Jorgito.

The next morning Guille avoided running into his brother. He knew his brother was angry. Therefore, his glass of milk remained untouched on the table. He did not dare to sit with the rest of his brothers. Jorgito took notice and decided to go in search for him.

He found him in his room with a ridiculous Lego construction in his hands.

"What's that, Guille?"

The little one, afraid, handed it over. It was a ridiculous ship made with a few pieces he found under the furniture.

"Have you tried to rebuild it?"

Guille nodded.

Jorgito looked at him until a smile escaped from his face.

"Well, if the Lord has forgiven our sins on the cross, I think I can forgive you for a ridiculous Lego ship. It is not a perfect love, but we must start somewhere."

Chapter Twenty

JORGITO AND THE TRIUMPH OF GOD[*]

*I have fought a good fight, I have finished my course, I have
kept the faith. Moreover, it is to me the crown of righteousness,
which the Lord, the righteous judge, will give to me on that
day; and not only to me but also to all who love his appearing.*

2 TIMOTHY 4:7-8

JORGITO's family had an intense Easter. They spent the
first days in the city in order to enjoy the processions
which the little ones loved so much. Jorgito continued
to be amazed by the Easter thrones. They were so beautiful! With each one that passed, Mamá and Papá explained
the episodes of the Passion to their children and so, between
drum beats and parades of penitents, the small ones learned
the mysteries of the Passion, Redemption, and Resurrection
of the Lord.

Jorgito wanted to be very close to the Lord that week and
took advantage of the fact that Papá had taken a few days
off work to pray before the tabernacle. He felt at home there
and made good use of his moments of prayer. Sometimes
they were too short!

At night time the parents had prepared a screening of
Easter movies. Jorgito liked all of them, but he had a special weakness for *Ben Hur*; so much so that Mamá assumed
that the next day her little ones would be holding endless
chariot-chair races throughout the hallway.

On Holy Wednesday, the family changed their focus and
sought refuge in the country house. They liked to retreat from

<hr>

*Story first published in *Adelante la Fe* on April 6, 2015.

worldly noise and live a peaceful Holy Office with Father Alfonso—advantages of rural retirement! Holy Thursday was cause of great celebration: it was the day of the institution of the priesthood. "We must pray so that God will send us good and holy priests!" exclaimed Mamá while she dreamed that one day she might see her sons donning cassocks. Good Friday: a day of fasting, penance, and prayer. Papá explained that this was a holy day and therefore the children must behave exceptionally well; it was a time for silence, meditation, and solitude. The parents took turns visiting the Altar of Repose in the morning and the two elder children decided to join them. Songs, jokes, and laughter were muted as formerly marked the tradition.

And finally the Easter Vigil arrived, which proved to be a great time for everyone. The family dressed in their finest clothes and enjoyed the solemn celebration Father Alfonso had prepared. When they arrived at the country house, a large banquet awaited them. Jesus Christ had risen! It was a time for joy!

Jorgito went to bed with an inflamed heart. His great Friend, Jesus, had triumphed; the cross remained naked, victory for mankind! He felt such joy that he rose from bed to give a last goodnight kiss to all the members of the family. Mamá and Papá laughed and returned the gesture with affection.

"I love you very much," he whispered as he went back to sleep.

Jorgito woke up in the middle of the night; something had interrupted his rest.

"Hello, Jorgito!" greeted Jesus.

"Lord!" replied a sleepy and confused child, "what are You doing here?"

"I've come for you. It's time for you to go with me," He announced lovingly.

"Where?" he asked, still groggy from sleep.

Christ smiled sweetly and responded, "To heaven."

Jorgito, now understanding His words, looked at Him deeply.

"I'm afraid, Lord."

"Why, Jorgito? I've been waiting for this moment from all eternity. Besides, look! Many familiar souls await you."

The child took a closer look and recognized many dear friends: Saint Dominic Savio, Saint John Bosco, Saint Francis, Saint Jerome, Saint Joseph... He instantly located a face in the background that captivated him; it was Mary, the Mother of God. They were all smiling at him.

"And my family?"

The Lord, anticipating the question, pointed behind Him. There Jorgito saw Papá, Mamá, and his four brothers. "The world is approaching hard times, Jorgito, and this family has already fulfilled its part. This is not your battle to fight."

Jorgito didn't understand Jesus' words, but he felt his heart was about to burst. This time without any fear, he reached his hand toward the Lord's. "Heaven is so beautiful...!" he muttered while his fingers touched Christ's.

The next morning, the world woke up to some tragic news on the radio: a family of seven was found dead in a house because of a carbon monoxide leak in the fireplace. The radio gave a few more details of the event, but immediately focused on other matters of interest such as the increase in public funding for Planned Parenthood, the slaughter of Christians in Syria, the rate of abortions in Spain, the ratification of new members for the Synod of the Family...

The whole city mourned the tragedy: There are things that can never be understood! They had a lifetime ahead! What a shame! No justice! Where was God...?

Days later, the grandfather, recollecting things left in the house, entered a room and found an object that caught his eye on the night table. *The Lord of the Rings*, the book which he had once read to his daughter when she was just a child, lay placid and oblivious to the terrible events that had happened days ago.

He recalled then that Mamá, as he had done once, was reading it to her offspring. Gently, he picked it up and discovered a page protected by a bookmark:

> "Yes, said Gandalf, "for it will be better to ride back three together than one alone. Well, here at last, dear friends, on the shores of the Sea comes the end of our fellowship in Middle-earth. Go in peace! I will not say: do not weep; for not all tears are evil."
>
> Then Frodo kissed Merry and Pippin and last of all Sam, and went abroad, and the sails were drawn up, and the wind blew, and slowly the ship slipped down the long grey firth, and the light of Galadriel that Frodo bore, glimmered and was lost [...]."

The grandfather wept a tear. He realized they had finished reading *The Lord of the Rings* that tragic night. And simultaneously, he understood that books have their own language and, when they are listened to, are able to scream to the soul. Mamá had left her farewell on the table and grandfather, in his old wisdom, had managed to decipher it.

"No, my children, certainly not all tears are bad," he said to himself, knowing that he had a priceless treasure in his jacket: the worn volume, a silent witness of his family's triumph.

www.ingramcontent.com/pod-product-compliance
Lightning Source LLC
Chambersburg PA
CBHW020617130626
46552CB00003B/1008